D0108616

CHARLIE BUMPERS vs.
HIS BIG BLABBY MOUTH

CHARLIE BUMPERS vs. HIS BIG BLABBY MOUTH

Bill Harley

Illustrated by Adam Gustavson

Ω

PEACHTREE

PUBLISHERS

Published by
PEACHTREE PUBLISHERS
1700 Chattahoochee Avenue
Atlanta, Georgia 30318-2112
www.peachtree-online.com

Edited by Vicky Holifield
Design by Nicola Simmonds Carmack
Composition by Melanie McMahon Ives

The illustrations were rendered in India ink and watercolor.

Printed in July 2017 in the United States of America by LSC Communications in Harrisonburg, VA
10 9 8 7 6 5 4 3 2 1
First Edition

Library of Congress Cataloging-in-Publication Data

Names: Harley, Bill, 1954- author. | Gustavson, Adam, illustrator.
Title: Charlie Bumpers vs. his big blabby mouth / written by Bill Harley ;
    illustrated by Adam Gustavson.
Other titles: Charlie Bumpers versus his big blabby mouth
Description: First edition. | Atlanta : Peachtree Publishers, [2017] |
    Summary: "With a little exaggerated bragging, Charlie convinces his
    classmates that his accountant dad would be the greatest Career Week
    speaker ever, and, using his friend Tommy's 'Parent Persuasion Strategy,'
    he finally talks his dad into coming. What could possibly go wrong with
    Charlie's plan?"— Provided by publisher.
Identifiers: LCCN 2016052237 | ISBN 9781561459407
Subjects: | CYAC: Fathers—Fiction. | Occupations—Fiction. |
    Schools—Fiction. | Humorous stories.
Classification: LCC PZ7.H22655 Cd 2017 | DDC [Fic]—dc23 LC record available at
https://lccn.loc.gov/2016052237

To Marken

Welcome to the clan

Contents

1

Almost the President

"Struggle of the Titans?" my best friend Tommy Kasten blurted out. "Your dad made up Struggle of the Titans?"

"Yeah yeah yeah," Alex McLeod said, his legs and head bobbing up and down. "With three other guys in his company."

"Best game ever!" Tommy started making ray gun noises like he was fighting a space alien.

"I've never heard of it," Ellen Holmes said.

"I can't wait for your dad to come in, Alex," Robby Rosen said. "Maybe he'll bring in free games for each of us."

"That would be awesome," said Hector Adélia, another one of my best friends.

"He can't," Alex said. "He's going on a business trip that week."

A bunch of us were sitting at lunch in the cafeteria talking about Career Week, which my fourth-grade class was having in two weeks. Every afternoon, parents would come in to talk to us about their jobs.

Ellen, Robby, Hector, and Alex were in Mrs. Burke's class with me. Tommy was in Mrs. Ladislavski's class (everyone calls her "Mrs. L.") and so was Tracy Hazlett, who was also sitting at our table.

"I hope Tricia's dad comes and brings stuff for us," I said.

"What's he do?" Alex asked.

"She told me he works for a company that makes all sorts of sports jerseys and hats. Maybe he'll bring everyone a hat."

"I wish *we* were having Career Week," Tommy

groaned. "Mrs. L.'s class always has Rainforest Week. No one ever gets jerseys or hats on Rainforest Week."

"Maria's parents run a bakery," Alex said. "Maybe they'll bring in something to eat."

"Oh, man, I *love* their bakery!" Tommy said. "Sometimes we get their cinnamon rolls on Saturday mornings. Maybe I could transfer to your class for the week."

"Charlie, what do your parents do?" Robby asked.

I hadn't asked my parents to come in for Career Week.

Mostly because I forgot.

My parents didn't design games or bake rolls or make jerseys and hats.

"My mom's a nurse," I said. "She visits people in their homes. My dad's an accountant."

"What's that?" Robby asked.

"He mostly works with numbers."

"He just sits around adding and subtracting numbers all day? That sounds really boring," Robby said, faking a big yawn.

"My dad's not boring." I glared at Robby. "He's... he's great at math."

"A math genius," Tommy added.

My best friend has a way of exaggerating things.

"Really?" Tracy Hazlett asked. "A genius?"

She smiled at me, which made my stomach very confused. I don't know why. I always have a hard time talking to Tracy Hazlett, which I don't want to talk about.

"Um, yeah," I said. "He's really smart. He makes a lot of decisions for his company."

"Like what?" Robby asked.

Actually, I didn't know what kind of decisions my dad made. I remembered once my dad told us that Mr. Jameson, the president of the company, had called him in for a private talk. I could tell my dad thought it was important.

"Big business stuff," I said. "Like when the

president needs to know something, he always asks my dad."

"Whoop-de-doo," said Robby. "Numbers are boring. My dad builds houses, and sometimes he lets me come and help him."

My dad had never asked me to help him at work. Sometimes he brought papers home and worked on his computer, but he'd never really showed me what he did.

"If my dad came in, you'd see how awesome he is," I said. "He's got a very important job."

"Like almost the president?" Tracy Hazlett asked.

"Well, almost," I said.

"Do you think your dad would really come in, Charlie?" Alex asked.

"I forgot to ask him. If Mrs. Burke still needs another parent, though, I bet he would."

"If he comes in, I hope he doesn't give us multiplication problems," Robby muttered.

"He'd be stupific," Tommy said. "Stupific" is a

word Tommy and I made up that means stupendous and terrific. "I've seen him do cool tricks with calculators."

"Calculators?" Alex asked. "Could he bring in calculators?"

Just then the buzzer sounded and lunch period was over. Everybody got up from the table, but I just sat there holding my milk carton, thinking about my dad and Career Week.

Tracy Hazlett smiled at me as she left. "I hope your dad gets to come speak to your class."

I tried to smile back, but my mouth twisted in a weird way.

"Let's go, Charlie," Tommy said. "Don't waste recess!"

I got up to follow the others, but I couldn't get my mind off my dad's job. What did he really do? I wondered if his boss Mr. Grimaldi would even give him the afternoon off to come into school. Maybe my dad *could* come in. And maybe he could do something cool. And maybe someday he'd be president of the company.

Or maybe not.

Sometimes I have a big blabby mouth.

2

I Am Math Genius

That night after dinner, my little sister Mabel (my dad calls her "Squirt" but I call her "the Squid" because it's funnier) was sitting at the kitchen table and my mom was quizzing her on addition. My sister's in first grade, so the problems were pretty easy, like 65 plus 11 and 73 plus 22. But she was still having a hard time.

Dad was washing the dishes. I was drying and putting things away.

"I don't like this," the Squid announced. "It's too hard."

Dad turned around.

He opened his eyes wide and stared at her. His mouth was sort of twitching. "No, math ees not hard," he said. "Ees bee-yoo-ti-ful."

A big smile broke out on the Squid's face. "Daddy, you're talking funny."

Sometimes Dad talks in a strange accent, like he's a mad scientist or something. Just to be weird. The accent isn't from any real country; it's just something he does to make us laugh.

"Wait beeg minute," he said. Then he opened the kitchen desk drawer and pulled out a deck of cards.

"Stop work immediately!" he shouted. "Important noomber lesson for all!" He sat at the table and pushed the flash cards and papers to one side.

I put down the dish towel and went over to watch. Dad knew a bunch of card tricks, and it was always fun to see what he was going to do.

Just then my brother Matt came in the kitchen. "What's going on?"

"Daddy's talking funny," the Squid said.

"He certainly is," Mom said, smiling as she pushed her chair back and folded her arms.

"So what else is new?" Matt's two years older than me, and sometimes he acts like everybody on the planet is a bozo except him. He leaned against the counter to watch.

Dad shuffled the cards twice and spread them out on the table face up in a long line, so we could

see part of every card. Then he tied a cloth napkin around his eyes so he couldn't see anything.

"Charlie, please to follow directions," he said. "Choose card, noomber between one and ten, but do not say noomber."

"Noomber?" the Squid asked.

"He means number," Matt said.

I chose a card—it was a six.

"Now, mooltiply by five! But still do not say noomber! I weel tell you noomber in head. I am genius."

"Okay," I said. Five times six was thirty.

Dad put his hands on his head like he was thinking really hard. "Ach! Lightning in brain! Add seex!" he ordered.

"Okay," I said. Thirty plus six made thirty-six.

"Now! Very important! Divide by two." Our dog Ginger nuzzled my dad's leg.

"Go avay, leetle doggie," Dad said. "You are bothering math genius!"

"Are you really a genius?" the Squid asked.

"But of course!" Dad said. "But genius can work only weeth silence! Please! Do you have noomber, Charlie?"

"Yep," I said. Thirty-six divided by two was eighteen.

"Hokey-dokey," Dad went on, still being weird. "Take individual digits in your noomber and add together. Very easy."

"What do you mean?" I asked.

"For instance, if noomber ees forty-three, add four and three together."

"It's not forty-three," I said.

"No arguing with genius! Just add."

Easy. The number in my head was eighteen. One and eight is nine. "What next?" I asked.

"Prepare to gasp. I weel try to find noomber in deck of cards."

"What's the number?" the Squid asked.

"Only Charlie knows for sure," Mom said.

"Charlie, tell me so I know!" my sister said.

I whispered "nine" in the Squid's ear.

Meanwhile, Dad moved his hands slowly over the deck of cards, then turned over the first card on one end. That made all the other cards in the line flip over like a wave across the table. Now all the cards were facing down except for one in the middle.

"Vat is noomber on card facing up?" Dad said.

Omigosh. It was a nine.

"Ees your noomber?"

"Yeah!" I said. "How did you do that?"

"I am math genius," Dad said with a big smile.

We all applauded. Even Matt, who had officially declared our parents to be totally uncool.

Then Dad turned to the Squid and stood behind her. He put both hands on her head. "And now, I put genius in *your* brain." He closed his eyes and squeezed her head. "There!" he said. "Now, you are math genius."

"I am?" the Squid squeaked.

"Yes, but only eef you practice adding every day."

"But that's what I was doing!' the Squid said.

"Then you will be extra-special math genius!"

That's when I remembered what Robby had said about my dad being boring. He wasn't boring at all! Maybe he *was* a genius.

But nobody would ever know, since Dad wasn't coming to Career Week.

3

My Hand Went Up All by Itself

POW! Mrs. Burke's fingers snapped and we all got quiet.

When Mrs. Burke snaps her fingers, everybody listens. She has the loudest fingers on the planet.

Even Alex got quiet, and he's noisier and crazier than I am.

By five times.

"Class Council is called to order," Mrs. Burke announced. "Time for new jobs for the next two weeks."

Mrs. Burke was holding a can filled with Popsicle sticks, each labeled with the name of a person in the class. When it's time to change jobs, she draws out a stick, reads the name, and lets that person choose almost any job they want, like Sweeper, Paper Monitor, Gardener, or Librarian. There was really only one job I'd ever cared about getting.

The best job in Mrs. Burke's Empire.

MASTER MESSENGER.

When you're Master Messenger, you get to deliver things anywhere in the school. Mrs. Burke might send you to ask Mr. Turchin the custodian for help, or ask you to bring back something from the library or the office or even the teachers' lounge. It means you get out of class and you're in the hallway all by yourself while everyone else in the whole school is stuck in their rooms suffering.

I had never gotten to be Master Messenger.

"Let's see which citizen chooses first today." Mrs. Burke reached into the can, pulled out a stick, and read the name. "Crystal, you choose first."

Boogers! She'd be sure to choose the job I wanted. I sent brain waves (like Buck Meson, my favorite superhero) in Crystal's direction:

Do not choose Master Messenger!

Do not choose Master Messenger!

Do not—

"I'd like to be Imperial Zookeeper," she said.

Yes! Thank you, Buck Meson!

The Imperial Zookeeper feeds the hamster and the tortoise and the hermit crab.

"Great, Crystal," Mrs. Burke said. "Put your name in the slot on the work chart."

I still had a chance to be Master Messenger. I sent my Buck Meson brain waves out toward Mrs. Burke:

Choose Charlie next!

Choose Charlie next!

She slowly pulled out a stick and held it in her hand. She looked at the stick again. This was torture!

"Samantha," she said.

Aaaaah! Not Samantha Grunsky!

Samantha sits behind me and is monstrously annoying. I looked at her. She had an evil smile on her face.

Oh no! I thought. *She knows I want to be Master Messenger and will choose it just to annoy me even more.*

"I want to be Majestic Gardener."

"NO!" I shouted before I realized what she'd said.

"You want to be Majestic Gardener?" Samantha asked, giving me a puzzled look.

"Yes—I mean no," I said. "I mean yes, but it's okay."

She shook her head at me like I was a total moron.

"Next." Mrs. Burke reached in the can for another stick. The Buck Meson brain waves were not working with Mrs. Burke. I looked down at my desktop and put my hands over my ears. I couldn't bear it. I squeezed my eyes shut.

I stayed like that until Hector, who sits next to me, poked me in the arm.

I lifted my head and saw Mrs. Burke pointing a stick at me. "Charlie, you're next," she said.

"Me?" I gasped.

"What would you like?" she asked.

"I'd like to be Master Messenger," I announced.

"No!" Sam Marchand groaned. So did Manny Soares. And Lydia Berman.

Everybody wanted to be Master Messenger.

Mrs. Burke snapped the class back to order.

"Okay, Charlie. Are you sure you'll do a good job?"

"Yes!" I said. "I'll be like Mercury!"

Mercury, the messenger for the Roman gods, was like a superhero before there were superheroes. He had wings on his feet and flew through the air. I could just picture it: me, zooming down the hall like a rocket, delivering messages to the gods!

Or at least to Mrs. Rotelli, the school principal.

Mrs. Burke frowned. "You do not need to be Mercury. No flying."

"I know," I said.

"What do you think is important about being Master Messenger?"

"Deliver the message quickly," I said. "Go right there and come right back, and don't get sidetracked. Oh yeah, and don't make noise in the hall."

"Yes," she said, "and…?" She waited for me to finish.

"No running!" Samantha called out, shooting her hand up and answering before I could say anything.

"I was going to say that," I muttered. What did Samantha Grunsky know about my job? She was just Majestic Gardener.

"Fine, Charlie," said Mrs. Burke. "I think you'll make a great Messenger. As long as you remember the rules of your job."

I walked over to the job chart, took my card down, and put it in the Master Messenger slot.

"Don't forget, Charlie," Mrs. Burke said. "No flying. And no running, either."

I nodded.

While other kids chose their jobs, I thought about being Master Messenger for the next two weeks.

Stupific. Completely stupific.

"We'll change over to the new jobs on Monday," Mrs. Burke announced. "And now, there's one more thing before we go home."

I wasn't thinking about one more thing. I was thinking about being Master Messenger.

"We have to talk about Career Week," Mrs. Burke said. "Thanks to all of you who took home

21

the forms I gave you the other day. And a special thank-you to everyone whose parents are coming in for Career Week. But I still need one more parent."

Before anyone else could speak or think or raise their hand, Alex leapt out of his seat.

"Charlie said his dad could come!" Alex said. "He's a genius!"

"Alex, please," Mrs. Burke said. "Sit down. He's Charlie's dad, not yours."

Ellen, who sits in front of me, turned around, smiled, and nodded her head. Robby was looking at me, too.

Before I knew what was happening, my hand went up all by itself.

"Yes, Charlie?" Mrs. Burke said.

"Um, my dad is an accountant. Maybe he could come in and talk about numbers."

"Okay, Charlie. That sounds great." Mrs. Burke beamed.

"Ugh," whispered Cory Filkins. "Not numbers!"

I ignored him. "Yeah. He's really good with

numbers and he knows all kinds of tricks you can do with them. And he's really important in his company."

"Like a president?" Joey Alvarez asked.

"Not exactly," I said. "But almost."

"Did you take the form about the Career Week visits home to your father?" Mrs. Burke asked.

"Um, no, not yet."

"Well, have him read the form right away. Tell him to e-mail me if he's interested."

"Okay," I said. I wasn't sure where the form was, but I thought I could find it.

"That can be your first message," Mrs. Burke said.

When we lined up to go to the buses, Alex asked me, "Charlie, do you think your dad could really bring in calculators for the class?"

"Calculators?"

"Yeah. You said he could do tricks with calculators. Remember? Maybe he could bring some in for us."

"Oh, right." I nodded. "Don't worry. He'll bring in something cool."

"I hope so," Robby said.

"Me too," Dashawn said.

"Awesome," Alex said. "I hope it's calculators."

I wasn't worried about the calculators yet. First, I had to get Dad to come.

4

Parent Persuasion Strategy

"I don't know, Charlie," Dad said. "Things are pretty hectic at the office right now."

I had waited until after dinner to ask Dad. He was in the family room reading a magazine, with no one else around. Sometimes when your brother and sister and mother get involved, things get complicated.

"Please, Dad? Mrs. Burke really needs another parent to volunteer."

"I don't think so, Charlie," Dad said. "And I don't think your friends would really want to hear me talk about my job anyway."

"Yes they would, Dad," I said. "They'd love it! You could show them how important numbers are."

He tilted his head and frowned.

"Please?"

"I'm sure Mrs. Burke can find someone else," he said. Then he looked back at his magazine, like he was finished talking to me.

"Come on, Dad, please!"

He lowered his magazine again. "Charlie, not now."

I could tell Dad was getting annoyed.

"Could you just think about it?"

"Okay. I'll think about it."

"Great," I said. "Just let me know when you decide."

"Charlie," Dad said, putting down the magazine. "Enough."

"Okay, okay," I said. I could wait until the morning for his answer.

As long as it was yes.

◆ ◆ ◆

Parents take FOREVER. I asked Dad the next morning whether he had decided. He said he hadn't.

"When *will* you decide?" I asked.

"When I decide!"

He said it in a way that let me know he wasn't going to decide right then.

"Hey, Charlie," Matt said, looking up from his cereal. "Never ask anybody anything before 8 a.m. You're being a pest."

I figured there was no use asking Dad again, at least not while Matt was in the room. I ate my cereal as fast as I could, grabbed my backpack, and headed to the bus stop.

On the bus, I explained my problem to Tommy. "I asked my dad, and he almost said no. Then he told me to stop asking him. But everybody in my class thinks he's coming."

Tommy thought for a moment. "Getting parents to agree to something they don't want to do is almost impossible. You need a plan."

It was surprising for Tommy to say that. I didn't think Tommy ever planned anything.

"What do you mean?"

"Get out a piece of paper and pencil. We need a 'Parent Persuasion Strategy.'"

"What's that?"

"A way to make them to do what you want."

That sounded good to me. I took a notebook and pencil out of my backpack.

"Now," Tommy said, "let's put down the different things you can do to get your way. We'll put them in order, according to how desperate you are."

"Like what?"

"Well, the first thing to do is just ask them really nicely."

"I did that already. It didn't work."

Tommy nodded. "I know. But just write it down to show that you tried it. What's next?"

"I don't know." I scribbled down the words "Ask nicely."

"Yes, you do. After that, you leave hints around the house for them to see. Like if it's Christmas and you want a bike, you draw a picture of a bike and put it up on the refrigerator. You don't have to say anything. It's just there."

"I don't need a bike. I need my dad to come in for Career Week."

"You could ask for a bike for me," Tommy suggested.

"Wait!" I said. "Mrs. Burke gave me a sheet

of paper for him to sign. I could leave it on the refrigerator, or on his bed or something." I wrote down "Leave hints."

"Perfect," said Tommy. "Now if that doesn't work, what's next?"

I thought for a second. "Well, I could ask Mom and try to get her on my side."

"Excellent! Ask the other parent. Write that down!" Tommy was getting pretty excited, and I was, too. I'd never actually made a list of all the different ways to get what you wanted.

"Okay, if the hints don't work, I'll talk to my mom. If she thinks Dad should do it, he doesn't have a chance."

"Even more excellent. But you have to be careful. If they talk to each other, they might realize you were trying to trick them. That's a disaster."

"Catastrophe," I agreed.

"Disastrophe," Tommy announced.

I laughed. "Disastrophe! Stupific!"

"What's next?" he asked.

"I'm running out of things to write down," I said.

"All right," he said. "I have the answer. If none of that works, I think you're going to have to go for an all-out attack."

"What do you mean?"

"Bug him until he *has* to say yes."

"What if he doesn't like being bugged?"

"Write it down anyway. Sometimes parents just get tired of being pestered and give up."

I wrote down "Bug him" and looked up at Tommy. "That'll be tricky," I said. "If I bug him too much, he'll get mad and I won't even be able to talk to him."

"Right!" said Tommy. "Which is why it might be better not to say anything at all. That's the next step."

"What?"

"Sulking. The Silent Treatment."

"What?"

"Don't say anything. Just wander around the house pouting and sighing and looking really unhappy."

"I've done that plenty of times," I said. "But they usually just tell me to stop pouting and sighing."

"I know," Tommy said. "Which is why you shouldn't do it unless you have to."

I added "The Silent Treatment" to the list. "Anything else?" I asked.

"Well, there is one more thing," Tommy said. "But only if nothing else works."

"What's that?"

"Get down on your knees and beg. Tell them you'll die if they don't say yes."

"I don't think I'll die."

"Maybe not," Tommy said. "But you've got to sound really desperate. I recommend you do it like this…"

He stood up just as our bus driver Mrs. Lima turned off the street into the driveway of the school.

He got a really worried look on his face, like he was about to cry. Then he flopped over, slamming his hands and arms and face on the bus seat. "I beg you! I beg you!" he wailed. "I throw myself upon the mercy of the court!"

Everyone turned and looked at us.

"Tommy, sit down!" Mrs. Lima called.

Tommy sat down.

"What does that even mean?" I asked.

"I saw it in a movie once, when they were going to put someone in jail. It worked for that guy. I tried it once when I wanted an ice cream. My dad laughed so hard that he bought it for me."

I wrote it down. We pulled into the school circle and I looked at the list.

1. Ask nicely
2. Leave hints
3. Ask other parent
4. Bug him
5. The Silent Treatment
6. Beg!

At the top of it all I wrote in big letters:

PARENT PERSUASION STRATEGY

"Stupific," I said. "Thanks, Tommy."

"No problem," he said. "I am a parent expert. I've lived with two of them my whole life."

I felt better. Now I had a plan.

5

A Hopeless Dweeb

As soon as I got home, even before I walked Ginger, I put the Parent Persuasion Strategy into action. I'd already tried the first step so I looked at the list to see what was next.

Step 2: Leave hints.

I knew Dad always went right to the refrigerator when he got home from work to get a glass of orange juice. I dug through my backpack until I found the crumpled-up sheet Mrs. Burke had given me about Career Week and smoothed out the wrinkles. The refrigerator door was plastered with family pictures, so I took a couple down and stuck the sheet right in the middle of the door with a magnet.

Dad couldn't miss it.

After I walked Ginger, I just kind of hung around the house waiting for Dad to get home. Mom was out visiting a patient. Dad usually gets home early on Friday, so I was there when he came in the back door.

"Hi, guys," he said, then walked right to the refrigerator and opened the door. He poured his juice and put the carton back.

He didn't even notice the Career Week sheet! How could he miss it?

When Dad went out to the garage, I grabbed the paper and took it up into his bedroom and put it on his chest of drawers. He always takes off his watch and puts stuff from his pockets on top of the chest, so I figured he would see it there.

When he went up to his bedroom, I sat on the stairs, pretending like I was doing nothing. He came back out in his everyday clothes and walked past me on the staircase.

"What are you up to, Charlie?" he asked.

"Nothing," I said.

"Okay," he said, then headed down the stairs.

I looked into his room. The note was exactly where I'd left it. He'd put his watch right on top of it!

I took the sheet of paper downstairs and put it on the chair in the family room where he always sits.

He'd *have* to see it there.

But even that didn't work! When he sat down, he just put the paper on the stack of magazines by his chair.

I must have put the Career Week sheet in a dozen places that day. No matter where I put it, he didn't seem to see it.

Are dads blind?

I was getting more desperate. It was time for the next steps in the Parent Persuasion Strategy.

That weekend I went through the entire list.

Step 3: Ask other parent.

When I asked Mom for help, she said it was up to Dad and that I should talk to him.

Thanks, Mom.

Step 4: Bug him.

I pestered Dad most of Saturday and he told me to calm down. Mom told me to leave him alone.

Step 5: The Silent Treatment.

All day Sunday I sulked. I was as silent as I could be. Wherever Dad was, I kept my head down and walked by him kind of slow, pouting and sighing. If he noticed, he didn't say anything about it.

Nothing was working!

Sunday night I went up into my room and looked at the list Tommy and I had made. There was only one option left.

Step 6: Beg!

I stood in front of the mirror in my room and practiced what Tommy had told me to say: "I throw myself upon the mercy of the court!"

It didn't sound very convincing. I tried again, this time a little louder. "I throw myself upon the mercy of the court!"

Then I knelt down and clasped my hands like I was pleading for my life.

"I THROW MYSELF UPON THE MERCY OF THE COURT!"

Matt opened my door. "What the heck are you doing?"

"Nothing," I said, scrambling to my feet. "Leave me alone." I knew Matt wouldn't help me.

"You are a hopeless dweeb," he muttered, then went back to his room.

I went in my closet where no one could hear me, closed the door, and practiced the line over and over again in the dark.

I throw myself upon the mercy of the court!

I throw myself upon the mercy of the court!

I figured I was ready. It was getting late, and I had to get Dad to say yes before I went to bed.

Matt's door was shut. He was probably doing his homework. The Squid was in the bathroom brushing her teeth.

It was time to beg for my life.

I scooted down the stairs. Mom and Dad were in the living room, watching some boring movie with people talking too much.

"Dad?" I said.

He picked up the remote and hit Pause.

"Yes?"

"It's about Career Week."

"Charlie," Mom said. "I told you to stop asking your father about this."

It was now or never.

"Dad! Please!" I went down on my knees and held my hands together in prayer. "Please, Dad, please! My life depends on it!"

Mom and Dad just stared at me, then looked at each other.

I collapsed on the floor.

"I throw myself upon the mercy of the court!"

I was facedown on the rug, not looking up. I said it again, as loud as I could.

"I THROW MYSELF UPON THE MERCY OF THE COURT!"

I waited for my dad to say something. That's when I heard someone coming down the stairs. It was Matt.

"You've got to be kidding!" he hooted. "This is hilarious."

All Matt's whooping brought the Squid downstairs, too.

I raised my head and looked around. Matt was in hysterics. Mom and Dad were looking at me like I had hatched from some prehistoric alien space egg.

"What's going on?" the Squid squealed, which she does when she gets excited.

"Charlie's begging for his life!" Matt said.

"Why?" the Squid asked.

Now Mom and Dad were laughing so hard they couldn't answer.

I felt like an idiot.

Finally Dad spoke. "You two go back upstairs while we talk to Charlie."

"I think I should be here," Matt announced.

"So do I," said the Squid.

"Upstairs," Dad said, pointing at the staircase. "Now."

"Rats," Matt said.

"Rats," the Squid said, copying her bozo brother. They left the room.

"Charlie," Dad said. "What about my going to Career Week is so important to you?"

"I just want you to be there," I said, which wasn't the complete truth but close enough.

"It must be more than that," Dad said. "Did something happen?"

"Um, not really, it's just that…"

I didn't want to explain. But Mom figured it out.

"Charlie," she said in her serious-mom voice (which I hate), "did you already tell Mrs. Burke that Dad would come?"

"What?" I said, which is what you say when you don't want to tell the complete truth.

"Did you tell Mrs. Burke that your father would come in?"

"Maybe. Kind of."

"And so she's expecting me?" Dad asked.

"Kind of. But mostly—" I stopped.

"What else?" Dad asked.

"Well..." I gulped. "I think the other kids are expecting you, too. Because I told them how good you were with numbers and everything. And how smart and funny you are. They really want you to come in so you can show them."

Dad rubbed his forehead like his brains hurt. I stood there, just wishing he would say yes.

"Charlie," Dad said in his serious-dad voice.

I hate that voice, too.

"Uh-huh?"

"You shouldn't say someone will do something without asking them—"

"I know, but—"

"Charlie, I'm tempted to say no just so you learn the lesson."

Oh no! I thought. *Not that! I HATE learning lessons!*

"But it seems pretty complicated now. So even though it really isn't a good time for me to do it, I'll come to your class."

I leapt up off my knees. I gave him a huge hug. Two hugs. Three hugs.

"Thanks, Dad. Thanks so much! It'll be great!"

"I don't know about that, but I'll do my best."

"It'll be great," I said.

Mom was shaking her head, but smiling a little. "Get your pajamas on," she said.

I turned and bounded up the stairs. Halfway up I thought about the other things I'd told the kids at school—about Dad almost being president, and about how he would bring in something cool to hand out. But it didn't seem like a good idea to bring that stuff up now.

One thing at a time.

6

My Big Blabby Mouth

First thing Monday morning I told Mrs. Burke my dad was definitely coming in.

She smiled. "Great, Charlie. That will be a wonderful addition to the week." She handed me a big envelope. "Now, I'd like you to take this down to the office."

Stupific! I'd forgotten about being Mrs. Burke's Master Messenger! This was going to be a great two weeks. I burst out the door.

"No running like Mercury!" she called.

Right. I slowed down.

Our school hallways are like a big square. The office is on the other side of the school from the fourth- and fifth-grade classrooms. You can either go one way, down the first- and second-grade hallway and by the cafeteria, or the other way, past the fifth-grade classes on our hall, and then by the third-grade and kindergarten classes and library. It's a little faster to go by the first- and second-grade classes, so I went that way.

I reached the end of our hallway and turned the corner to the first- and second-grade wing.

I looked down the hall. No one in sight!

No running like Mercury! Mrs. Burke had said.

But then I thought about my favorite superhero, Buck Meson. In one episode, he had special rockets on his feet. It was unbelievable how fast he went. He approached the speed of light.

Mercury didn't show up in the hallway.

But Buck Meson did.

"Rockets engaged," I whispered to myself.

I flew down to the office in record time—the

fastest and best messenger in the history of King Philip Elementary School.

I delivered the package, then flew back, skidding to a stop right before I got to my classroom.

Rockets off!

Perfect. Mission accomplished!

I walked in slowly, hands in my pockets. Mrs. Burke was busy and didn't notice as I slipped into my seat.

"That was fast," Hector said.

"Just call me Buck Meson," I said, giving him a big grin.

"If anyone catches you running in the hall," Samantha hissed, "you'll lose your job."

I ignored her.

Mrs. Burke looked up and saw me back at my desk. "Did everything go all right?" she asked.

"Yes, ma'am," I said.

"No running?"

"No, ma'am," I said. (Which was true. I was *flying*.)

"Good for you," she said.

I turned and grinned at Samantha. She rolled her eyes and flipped her hair back like she couldn't care less. But Samantha flips her hair when something bothers her. I guess that something was me.

◆ ◆ ◆

At lunch that day, Robby Rosen started bugging me about my dad coming in. "What's your dad going to do, anyway? I hope it won't to be too boring."

"Don't worry," I said. "It definitely won't be boring."

"But what does he do? Will he bring in something for us?" Robby asked.

"Yeah," Joey chimed in, "like Maria's parents bringing in cookies?"

"Or Tricia's dad bringing in baseball caps?" Robby said.

"I don't know yet."

"What about bringing in calculators?" Alex asked.

"I'm not sure about that," I said. "He might."

"If he's the president of the company, he could," Joey said. "The president can decide what he wants and just do it."

Tommy and Hector sat there, quiet as mice. I'd never told either of them that my dad was president or anything like that. "I didn't say he was president," I said.

"I thought you did," Sam said.

"I said he's really important, like *almost* the president."

"That means calculators for everyone!" Alex shouted, spinning in circles on his seat. "Sweet!"

Everybody at our end of the table nodded. Even Tommy and Hector.

"We'll see," I said. Which in adult language means "I hope you forget."

I never should have said anything about my dad.

Me and my big blabby mouth.

7

At Least Vice President

We were almost done with dinner, and I had to ask Dad about the calculators. Very carefully.

"Hey, Dad," I said in my most polite voice.

"Yes?" He looked at me suspiciously.

"You use a calculator at work, right?"

"You know I do, Charlie. I work in numbers all day and I can't do everything in my head."

"Yeah, I know. I was just wondering, are there a lot of calculators at work?"

"Everybody in my department has one."

"Are there extras?"

"Sounds like Charlie wants a new calculator," Matt sang out.

Boogers. I'd forgotten one of the most important rules of being a kid: If you want something from your parents, don't ask when your big brother is in the room.

"No, I don't," I said, glaring at Matt.

"Then what *do* you want, Charlie?" Dad asked.

"When you come in to my class, are you going to do some of those tricks on the calculator that you showed us?" I asked. "You know, like the one where you can make it show all 9s?"

"I could do that," he said.

"Well, some of the kids might not have a calculator."

"So I should bring some they could borrow?"

"Um...are there any extras you don't need?" I asked.

"You mean that the kids could keep?"

I nodded my head hopefully.

"That is ridiculous," Matt said.

"Can I have a calculator, too?" the Squid asked.

"You know I can't do that, Charlie," Dad said.

"Oh," I said. "Okay."

"Let's have dessert," Mom said.

◆ ◆ ◆

After dinner, up in my room, I started thinking about this time when I was about five years old. My mom told me that I couldn't have ice cream unless I ate my green beans, so I told her that I would never speak to her again. Which, of course, was impossible. You can't stay mad at your mom forever. For one thing, you could starve to death.

I still remember what my Grandpa Al said to me that day: *Charlie, always think before you open your mouth. If you don't, you might put your foot in it, and once your foot's in there, it's hard to get it out.*

I didn't understand what he meant. But I do now. You have to be careful about what you say, because later you might just wish you hadn't said it.

Like all those things I'd said at school about my dad and his job.

I looked at my foot and wondered if I could really put it in my mouth.

I tried. I could only get my toes in.

I needed to talk to Dad again about bringing something to class, but not until Matt and the Squid weren't around.

When I heard them go to their rooms, I sneaked down the stairs so they wouldn't hear me. I even

remembered to step over the fourth stair from the bottom, the one that squeaks really loud. Mom and Dad were in the kitchen, so I made a detour through the living room.

Standing outside the door to the kitchen, I could hear them talking. They weren't quite whispering, but they were keeping their voices low, the way they did when they didn't want us to hear them.

"What did Grimaldi say?" Mom asked.

"He said I should have done it his way. He knew I was right, so he couldn't argue with me. But he really didn't like it."

Then it was quiet.

I stood really still.

What were they talking about? It had to be something about Dad's work. Mr. Grimaldi was Dad's new boss. I knew he and my dad didn't get along. But whatever it was, it sounded like Dad had done the right thing.

"So," Mom said, "do you want to guess what's going to happen?"

"I've got an appointment to talk with Jameson," Dad said.

Jameson! Mr. Jameson's the president of the company!

"Really?" Mom asked.

"Yeah. I don't think things will stay the same. The whole company is going through some changes. Either I get a promotion, or, well, you know…"

"Mmm-hmm." Mom paused for a second, then said, "Either way will be fine, Jim."

I heard a chair scrape back from the table, so I tiptoed away from the kitchen door as fast as I could and scooted back up the stairs. I lay down on my bed and tried to make sense of what I had overheard.

A promotion means you move higher up in the company and get paid more money.

I thought about that for a minute.

Dad must have solved a really hard problem that his boss couldn't solve. Maybe Mr. Jameson is going to retire and ask him to be president! Dad's really smart. And he's really good at numbers. He would make a great president! Or at least vice president.

Vice president would be enough, I decided. Vice presidents would have a lot of calculators. That would make sense—the higher up you got, the more calculators you needed.

Maybe even enough for my whole class.

8

Rockets on My Feet

Mrs. Burke called me up to her desk on Tuesday morning. "Charlie, I haven't heard from your father. I need to get that sheet from him."

Uh-oh. The sheet she gave me. Where was it? I'd moved it around the house so much trying to get my dad to see it, I'd lost track of it.

"Um...I think I might need another one."

Mrs. Burke shook her head, then opened a drawer and pulled out a folder. "Don't lose this one," she said, handing me a new copy. "My e-mail address is there, and so is my phone number. Please ask your father to get in touch with me."

"I think he might be getting a promotion," I blurted out.

Mrs. Burke's face broke into a big smile. "Well, that's wonderful to hear. You must be very proud of him."

I nodded. "He's really smart. He can do a lot of fun things with numbers."

"I'm sure he can. And I'm eager to have him come in and share."

I started back to my seat.

"Wait, Charlie," Mrs. Burke said, holding up a manila folder with a big rubber band around it. "Would my messenger please take this to Mrs. Finch in the office?"

Stupific! Another errand! "Sure!" I said.

"Deliver it and then come right back," she said.

I took the folder and headed out the door. I walked to the near end of the fourth- and fifth-grade wing, then turned at the corner to go by the first- and second-grade classes.

The hallway was quiet—everyone was in class except me.

When I got to the first-grade classes, I saw that Mrs. Diaz's door was open. I slowed down to look for the Squid.

She saw me first. "Hi, Charlie!" she shouted. "Hey, everybody, there's my brother!"

"Mabel!" I heard Mrs. Diaz say.

I waved to the Squid but kept going. Disrupting a class is a bad idea, since sometimes teachers talk to each other. I didn't want Mrs. Burke to find out that her Master Messenger had wandered off course. When I got to the office I held out the folder to Mrs. Finch, the secretary.

"This is from Mrs. Burke," I said.

"Thanks, Charlie," she said.

Our principal, Mrs. Rotelli, stuck her head out of the office. "Hello, Charlie," she said. "Are you the new messenger for Mrs. Burke's Empire?"

"Yes, ma'am."

"Wait just a minute," she said. "I have another

delivery for you." She went back in her office and came out with a big brown envelope. "Please give this to her."

"Okay," I said.

"Thanks, Charlie!" she called as I headed back toward my classroom.

I got to the first-grade classes. The hallway was long and quiet. No one was in sight. The doors were all closed—I guess Mrs. Diaz had shut hers when the Squid called to me. I imagined what it would be like to have rockets on my feet. I could almost hear them revving up, getting ready to take off.

Vrummm-vrummmmmm.

At first I only jogged a little. Would Buck Meson be late with the delivery?

I DON'T THINK SO!

I sped up. *WHOOOOSH!*

I zoomed by the second-grade classes.

I was almost to the end of the hallway when the adult bathroom door opened up in front of me.

Mr. Turchin, the custodian, came out wheeling a

big cart with a garbage can and a mop bucket on it.

I screeched to a halt, almost running into him.

"Whoa!" he said. "Where's the fire?"

"I'm Mrs. Burke's Master Messenger," I said.

"Well, Mr. Messenger, do you want to take these down to Mr. Araujo's class?" he asked, holding out a big stack of paper towels. "He said he needs them pronto."

"Sure," I said. "I know where it is. It's just a little past my classroom." Mr. Araujo was a fifth-grade teacher on the other side of the hall from ours.

"Thanks, Charlie," he said. "I can always count on you."

I took the paper towels and turned the corner, accelerating to the end of the hallway.

I had a job to do. I accelerated a little more.

Buck Meson engaged the afterburners.

HWWWEEEEEEEE! The jet engines were roaring. Classrooms flew by.

Mrs. Burke stepped out of our classroom door.

EMERGENCY! EMERGENCY!

ABORT MISSION! ABORT MISSION!

I slammed on the reverse rockets. Too late.

Mrs. Burke folded her arms and screwed up her mouth. "Where have you been?"

"The office," I said, which was true. I was breathing hard from running, but trying not to show it.

"What are those?" she asked, nodding at the towels.

"Paper towels. Mr. Turchin asked me to take them to Mr. Araujo's class," I gasped. "He needs them pronto. And this envelope is for you...from Mrs. Rotelli." I handed it to her.

"Charlie, what were you doing just then?" she asked.

"What?" I sputtered.

"Were you running or walking?"

Trick question! No good answer!

"Um...trying to get back to class in a hurry?"

"Were those rockets I heard?"

"Um, maybe."

Mrs. Burke pointed down the hallway with her long, firecracker-snapping finger. "Take the towels to Mr. Araujo's class and come straight back. Don't dawdle."

"Okay," I said.

"But walk."

The ruler of Mrs. Burke's Empire was not happy. The Master Messenger was going to have to be more careful if he didn't want to lose his job.

9

There Are Dinosaurs in My Pot

Right after lunch on Wednesday we had art with Ms. Bromley. I like art because you can talk while you're working on something without worrying about Mrs. Burke's exploding fingers.

You never know what Ms. Bromley is going to wear. There are always weird buttons and pins hanging off her shirts or sweaters, and sometimes she wears striped leggings and extra bands in her hair. Ms. Bromley is a walking art exhibit all by herself.

I was sitting at a table with Hector, Joey, Alex, and Ellen. We were making collages from different pieces of colored tissue paper. Ellen's was a vase of flowers. Hector's was a seaside landscape.

Mine was supposed to be Buck Meson's spaceship, but something had gone terribly wrong. It looked more like the losing car at a demolition derby. I grabbed another sheet of tissue paper and tore it into strips.

"Hey, Charlie. What day is your dad coming in?" Alex asked.

"Next Friday," I said.

"My mom's coming in on Wednesday," Ellen said. "She works at home and designs web pages, and she's going to help us work on one for our class."

"Mrs. Burke will love that," Joey said. "The Empire will have its own official web page."

"Yeah," I said. "That would be great."

"Do you know what kind of calculators your dad is bringing in?" Joey asked.

"Um, no."

Robby Rosen came over from another table. "What are you guys talking about?" he asked.

"We're talking about Charlie's dad bringing in calculators for our whole class," Alex said.

"No way," said Robby.

"*Yes* way," Alex interrupted.

"You're crazy," Robby said. "That would cost a lot of money. Is your dad a millionaire, Charlie?"

Everyone looked at me.

"No," I said.

"Well, what is he?"

"He's not a millionaire. But I think he might be getting a promotion."

"Like president of his company?" Ellen asked.

Before I could answer, Sam came over. "What's going on?"

"Charlie's dad's bringing calculators for our class, maybe even for the whole fourth grade!" Joey crowed.

"Awesome!" Sam said.

"You're all full of baloney," Robby said.

"Charlie's dad is going to be president," Alex explained. "So he can get as many calculators as he wants. Right, Charlie?"

"Wait, you guys," I said, shaking my head. "I didn't say that."

"Well, I sure hope he does," Alex said. Now there were six kids all talking about my dad.

That's when I remembered playing Telephone in Mrs. Crandall's second-grade class. Mrs. Crandall loved quiet, so it was her favorite game. First she'd have us all sit quietly in a circle. She'd whisper a sentence into the first kid's ear, and then one person after another would whisper the sentence they'd heard to their neighbor. At the end, the first person would say the original words aloud, and the last person would call out the sentence he had just heard. They were never the same. You could start out with a sentence like "My dog's name is Spot" and the last kid might say, "There are dinosaurs in my pot," and everyone would laugh.

Now my life had turned into a giant game of

Telephone. I had said one thing, and everybody had heard something else.

I wanted everyone to be excited about my dad's visit, and I didn't want them to be disappointed. But things were getting crazy.

I thought about standing on top of the table and announcing to everyone that my dad was DEFINITELY NOT PRESIDENT AND THAT HE WOULDN'T BE HANDING OUT FREE

CALCULATORS! But they were all back in their seats. I hoped they'd eventually just forget about it.

I was wrong.

At the end of the day, when I was about to get on the bus, Tracy Hazlett came up to me.

"Hi, Charlie," she said.

"Hi," I mumbled. Which was the best I could do around Tracy Hazlett.

"I heard your dad is bringing in calculators for your class."

"Um, I, uh…maybe."

"Do you think there might be an extra one? For me?"

"Um, sure," I said. It was hard to say no to Tracy Hazlett.

"Great!" She gave me a big smile and walked away.

Why did I say that?

I just stood there like a huge, moronic bozo. Missy Blair, a girl from one of the other fourth-grade classes, came over and stood in front of me.

"Must be nice to have a dad with a private jet for his business," she said, then left before I could say anything.

How did we get from my dad the math genius to my dad the high-powered millionaire flying around in his own plane?

This game of Telephone was completely out of control!

◆ ◆ ◆

That night when I was looking for my homework assignment, I pulled out a sheet of paper that said "Information for Guests on Career Day" across the top.

Oh no! I was supposed to give it to my dad yesterday! I hurried downstairs and found him sitting in his favorite chair, reading a book.

"Dad, here's the sheet from Mrs. Burke about Career Week."

He took the paper, read a few lines, then looked up at me. "Are you sure you want me to do this, Charlie?"

"Yeah. I told Mrs. Burke you were coming. You're supposed to call her."

He read the rest of the note.

"Wow," he said. "This is like a homework assignment. She sure is organized."

"I know," I said. "She's the most organized person on the planet."

"Okay," he said. "I guess I'd better send her a note."

"So, Dad," I said. "If you come, what will you do?"

"I'll have to think about it," he said, looking back at his book.

I thought about his promotion. "Um, is there anything new at work?"

He lowered the book and gave me a strange look. "Why do you want to know?"

"Just wondering," I said. "Just wanted to know how you were doing."

"How I'm doing?"

"I mean…how's Mr. Grimaldi?"

My dad frowned. "Mr. Grimaldi is fine, thank you."

"Do you think *he* might have any extra calculators?"

"No, Mr. Grimaldi does not have any extra calculators. If you need a new calculator, Charlie, just—"

"No," I said quickly. "Just wondering."

"Don't you have homework?"

"Yes."

"Then go finish it. Now. Don't wait around until it's almost bedtime."

"Okay, but—"

"Now."

"Okay," I said, heading toward the stairs.

Boogers.

10

Even the First Graders!

I'm happy to announce that Buck Meson did not get caught flying down the halls on Thursday. Or Friday.

Buck Meson did have his rockets on, but he was so fast nobody even noticed him. It's hard to see someone traveling at the speed of light.

I ran when no one else was in the hall—but NEVER near Mrs. Burke's Empire.

While Buck Meson was flying, the game of Telephone was getting worse and worse. The stories about my dad were getting bigger and bigger. Now everybody was talking about free calculators, and some kids were asking if my dad could come to their class, too.

A third grader asked me if my family used my father's jet when we went on vacation.

Another boy I didn't know asked me if my dad had more than one jet.

One kid from Mrs. L.'s class said he hoped my dad got to be president of the company so the school would get new computers.

Even Darren Thompson and Kyle Curtis started being nice to me. When Darren Thompson is nice to me, something is definitely weird. I guess they figured that if there was any chance my dad would be handing out free calculators, they'd better quit bugging me all the time and get on my good side.

Everything was weird. All the kids were excited about my dad coming in. That felt good. It made me excited, too.

But what would happen when he came in?

And he didn't have a jet plane.

And he wasn't the president.

And he didn't have calculators.

What if he was just a dad that was good with numbers and worked every day?

Shouldn't that be enough?

◆ ◆ ◆

That Friday afternoon, Mrs. Burke reminded us about Career Week. "We'll have one parent coming in every afternoon next week," she said. "I want you to be respectful—they are giving up time from their important jobs to be with us. And one more thing," Mrs. Burke said. "Do not expect any of our guests to bring in special gifts for you."

Maria Braxton raised her hand. "My parents run a bakery," she said. "They promised they'd bring in some cookies."

Everybody cheered.

"That's very nice, Maria," Mrs. Burke said. "But it doesn't mean everyone is going to bring in something."

Mrs. Burke wasn't looking at me, but half a dozen kids were. I could feel my ears turning red.

When I glanced over at Hector, he shook his head and cleaned off his glasses, which he always does when he doesn't know what to say or do.

If I'd had glasses, I would have cleaned them off, too.

◆ ◆ ◆

The Squid and I got off the bus and walked toward our house.

"Charlie," the Squid said, "somebody asked me if our dad was president of the United States."

"*What?*"

"Cameron Benson said he heard from his sister that our dad was president."

"No!" I said. "Not president of the United States! She probably meant president of the company."

"Is he?"

"No! He's just an accountant. He's good at numbers. That's all. That's enough!"

"Then why did his sister say that?"

"Listen, Mabel, it's just a story. But don't say anything about it to Dad, okay?"

"Where'd the story come from?"

"Somebody misunderstood me," I said. "So just forget it."

"Will Dad ever be the president of something?" Now the Squid was really interested.

"I don't know!" I said. "Just forget it."

"Okay, okay!" she said. "Don't be so crabby."

How could I not be crabby? Now even the first graders were talking about my dad.

11

A Big Poopbrain

When the Squid and I walked in the back door, Mom and Dad were sitting at the kitchen table with Matt. I could tell right away something was wrong. It was Friday afternoon, so Dad should have been at work and Mom should have been out visiting patients.

Maybe Matt had done something bad at school. Once when he was in fourth grade, he pulled the fire alarm and my parents were called in to talk with Mrs. Rotelli. Mom and Dad were so mad they didn't speak to any of us during dinner that night.

Or maybe it was something good. Something

so good everyone was serious! Like if he was made president of the company, you'd have to be serious. It was very important.

For a split second, I had a picture in my mind of him bringing hundreds of calculators to school—enough for every person at King Philip Elementary School.

But Dad didn't seem very happy. You should be happy if you were going to give away four hundred calculators.

"Why is everybody here?" the Squid asked.

It got quiet for a minute. Even Matt, who always has something to say, just sat there looking down at the table.

"Why are you home, Daddy?" the Squid asked again.

"Well, Squirt, I'm home because I'm not going to be working at my old job anymore."

What? What does he mean?

Mom put her hand on Dad's arm.

"Why not?" the Squid squeaked.

"Well," Dad said, "the people who run the company made some changes, and they had to let several people go. I was one of them."

"Let you go where?" the Squid went on. "If you're not there, who's going to do your job?"

"Honey," Mom said, "I know you have a lot of questions, but we can't answer all of them right now. Right now we're just going to be happy that Daddy's home with us."

"Is he going to go work somewhere else on Monday?" The Squid's bottom lip started quivering.

"No," Dad said. "I'll be here. So it's pancakes for breakfast before school."

"And we're telling you all so we can go through this together," Mom said. "But listen, please—we're not talking about this with anyone else right now. Dad can do that when he's ready. Do you understand?"

Matt nodded.

The Squid pretended to zip her lips.

"Did Mr. Grimaldi fire you?" I asked.

"Charlie," Mom warned.

Dad took in a deep breath, like he was about to try to explain something. But I was getting really mad at Mr. Grimaldi.

"It's not fair!" I shouted. "He shouldn't fire you just because you do something better than he does!"

Mom and Dad looked surprised—they didn't know I'd overheard them talking the week before.

And then I realized something. When Dad was talking about "the other thing" that day, he was talking about losing his job! Mom had said it would be okay. How was that okay?

"Mr. Grimaldi's a total jerk!" I said.

"Charlie," Mom said.

My dad gave me a twisted smile. "It's more complicated than that, Charlie."

"He's a big *poopbrain*," the Squid blurted out. "You should fire *him!*"

Matt didn't say anything. He just kept looking at the table.

Then I realized something else. Forget what all

the other kids at school were expecting from my dad. Now he didn't even have a job!

"Dad," I burst out, "if you don't have a job, then how can you talk to my class during Career Week?"

"Charlie, we can't worry about that right now," Mom said.

"But Mrs. Burke is expecting you, Dad," I said. "And everyone else is, too." I didn't mention that practically the entire school thought he was a president with a private plane and a million free calculators.

"We'll see," Dad said.

All of a sudden I imagined Darren and Kyle and Robby and all the other kids laughing at me. "But what's going to happen? What will I tell everybody?"

"Charlie, stop it," Mom said, shaking her head at me. "This is not about you right now."

"It's okay," Dad said. "I understand. We'll figure something out."

"Yeah, but—"

"Shut up, Charlie," Matt said. That was the first

thing he'd said since I'd come home from school.

"Matt," Mom snapped. "We don't say 'shut up' in this house."

"Charlie, close your mouth right now," Matt said.

I could feel my throat tighten up, and tears welled up in my eyes.

"Dad, are we going to be poor?" the Squid asked.

"No, Squirt," he said. "We're fine."

The Squid dropped her backpack and went over to Dad and threw her arms around his neck. "I love you, Daddy," she said. "And Mr. Grimaldi is a big, big poopbrain."

"Name-calling doesn't help," Dad said.

"It helps me," the Squid said.

She was right. Calling Mr. Grimaldi a poopbrain *did* help a little. But it didn't help one bit with my problems at school.

◆ ◆ ◆

That night Mom and Dad came in and said good night to me. After Dad left, Mom stayed at the side of my bed. Then she leaned over and kissed my head.

"It'll be all right, Charlie," she whispered.

"I know," I said. And then she left.

But I didn't know. I lay there in bed, staring at the ceiling. I couldn't stop all the thoughts buzzing around in my head. Why did Dad lose his job? Because Mr. Grimaldi didn't like him? Why did he do the thing that made Mr. Grimaldi mad? What if I talked to the president of the company and explained how smart Dad was? Could he get his old job back?

Then I started thinking about what the Squid had said about being poor. If Dad didn't have a job, he wouldn't be getting paid. Would Mom have to work more to make more money? Could we still live in our house? What if I had to change schools? Would I still see Tommy? And Hector?

And then I had an idea. I sat up in bed.

What if Dad got a new job right away? An even better one, at another company? Maybe he could get a new job before he came in on Friday. Who knows, maybe he could even start his *own* company! I wouldn't care about calculators anymore if Dad had a new job. Far away from Mr. Grimaldi, the poopbrain.

That would solve everything. I would ask him about it tomorrow. I fell asleep thinking about Dad's new job.

◆ ◆ ◆

On Saturday morning, Dad was out doing errands by the time I got up. Nobody said anything about his job, but I could tell everybody was thinking about it. All weekend I kept looking for a time to talk to Dad, but I didn't get a chance until I went to bed on Sunday night. He came into my room to say good night. He sat on my bed and scratched my back, which always feels good.

"Dad?"

"Yeah?"

"Are you going to get a new job?"

"Of course."

"What is it going to be?"

"I'm not sure yet."

"Do you think you'll get it tomorrow?"

Dad shook his head. "No, Charlie, I won't get a new job tomorrow."

"Can you get one this week?"

"I doubt it."

"Do you think when you get a new job, you might be a vice president or something?"

"I don't think so," he said.

Then we both were quiet for a minute. Finally I got up the courage to ask another question. "Dad, I know this isn't about me, but what will you do if you come to my class on Friday? If you don't have a job, what will you say?"

"I don't know, Charlie. I'll think of something."

Then he leaned over and gave me a hug and a kiss on the head. "I love you, pal. Good night."

"Good night," I said.

He got up and gently closed the door behind him.

12

In Really Bad Shape

Monday afternoon Maria Braxton's mom showed up right on schedule. She was wearing a white apron and one of those big poufy chef's hats. She was also carrying a computer bag and two very large, flat brown boxes. The room filled up with the smell of a bakery.

Mrs. Braxton set her computer on a desk and hooked it up to the projector, then turned it on. In a few seconds, some words appeared on the big screen.

What Does a Baker Do?

"I've been a baker all my life," she said. She clicked and a picture of a little girl holding a tray of cupcakes came up. "That's me when I was only seven years old. I still make those cupcakes today. It's still one of my favorite recipes."

"Oh wow!" said Alex. "I'm already hungry!"

"And here are some of the other things I bake," she said.

She started a slide show of all kinds of breads and cakes and rolls and cookies.

"I'm dying!" Manny Soares moaned. "I want to be a baker!"

"But here's the first thing you need to know about being a baker," Mrs. Braxton went on. "You have to go to bed really early. This is the first thing I see every morning." The next picture showed an alarm clock that said 3:00 a.m.

"This is when I get up every day," she said.

"Forget being a baker!" Manny said.

"I'll be a professional eater," Sam suggested. "Can you get paid for that?"

Mrs. Braxton went through the rest of her pictures, showing all the things she did during the day. Who knew baking was so complicated?

"There's a lot of math involved," she said. "I do a lot of measuring, and I also have to keep track of the business, so I do all the orders and accounting."

Tricia Davidoff raised her hand. "Charlie's dad's an accountant, too."

"He's President of Accounting!" Cory shouted.

"He's King of Numbers!" Alex added.

"He has a million calculators," Joey hooted.

"Well," Maria's mom said. "He's a very good person to know! We all need math."

Everyone looked at me and smiled. I felt like throwing up.

"Now," Maria's mom said, "I think it's time to taste my work." Mrs. Braxton opened up the boxes and the smell of fresh cake and icing spread across the room.

"If you can be quiet for a few minutes, we'll get started. I brought enough for everyone," she said. "Line up, take a napkin, and help yourselves."

We all got up and stood in line. Even Mrs. Burke.

"This is the best Career Week talk ever," someone said.

Josh Little was right in front of me. He's always very kind and polite and thoughtful, which is probably why he turned and said, "Don't worry, Charlie. When your dad hands out calculators, the kids are going to like his presentation even more."

I just nodded. What could I say? I took my cupcake and sat at my desk, staring at it. When you don't feel like eating cupcakes, you're in really bad shape.

◆ ◆ ◆

Dad was waiting for us in the kitchen when the Squid and I got home. "Want to walk Ginger together?" he asked me.

"Sure," I said. Sometimes Dad walked Ginger around the block when I couldn't do it, but we hardly ever did it together.

He stuffed a plastic bag in his pocket for you-know-what, or as my dad says, "the call of nature."

Or as I say, "poop."

"Are you picking it up?" I asked.

"No. I'll carry the bag, but *you* have to pick it up. You're closer to the ground than I am."

"That's not fair," I said.

"Life's not fair," he said, smiling.

Ginger led us on our usual route around the

block. We stopped for a minute and said hi to Mrs. Lapidus while her dog Lovey-Doodle (That's his name. I'm not making it up.) yapped at Ginger.

Ginger strained to get at the little mutt, but I pulled on her leash until she gave up and started walking again.

Dad asked me about school and I told him about my job as Mrs. Burke's Master Messenger. I explained how I was like Buck Meson except I wasn't supposed to run.

"Do you ever run when no one's looking?" he asked.

"Sometimes," I said.

"I figured," he said. "I know you."

At the cat lady's house we saw her two cats Alice and Gertrude looking out of the front window. Ginger tried to lunge at them, but I jerked her back onto the sidewalk. Just as we made the turn for home, we saw Mr. Gritzbach out in his front yard smoking a cigar. He's kind of a grumpy old guy, and he's always worried about Ginger pooping in his yard.

"Hi, Raymond," Dad said to him.

"Hello, Jim." He scrunched up his bushy gray eyebrows like he was trying to figure something out. "You taking the day off?"

Uh-oh. I looked at Dad. *What is he going to say to Mr. Gritzbach?*

Dad took in a deep breath, then let it out all at once. "Yep. Just taking a little time off."

"Well, enjoy yourself," Mr. Gritzbach grumbled.

"I'll try," Dad said.

When we were almost home, Dad put his arm around my shoulder. "It's nice walking with you."

"I like it, too." I really did, but I also couldn't hold in my questions anymore.

"Dad?"

"Yeah?"

"Did you look for a new job today?"

"Not today," he said. "I thought about it a lot, though."

Thought about it? Why can't he just go find one?

"Oh," I said. Though I wanted to say a lot more.

13
Putting Your Foot in Your Mouth

The next morning, I didn't feel any better. There was plenty of work to do, but I couldn't concentrate. Sam Marchand's dad was coming in that afternoon to talk about being an electrician, and Sam was bragging about it, which drove me crazy.

I felt like the terrible secret I had was too big to keep to myself.

Who could I tell without worrying that they'd blab to someone?

I knew. Tommy and Hector.

After lunch, when we went out onto the playground, I stopped both of them before we got to the soccer field. "You guys," I said. "Wait!"

"We gotta hurry, Charlie," Tommy said. "We have to be there to choose up sides."

"Just a minute," I said.

"What is it?" Hector asked.

I couldn't tell them yet. There were too many kids around.

"Over here." I led them to the corner of the playground behind the slide. A couple of second graders were climbing on it, but no one really noticed us.

"What's wrong?" Tommy whispered.

"I'm not supposed to say," I said. "You have to really, really promise not to tell anyone."

Tommy looked curious. Hector looked worried.

"I mean it, you have to swear," I said.

"Cross my heart, hope to die," Tommy pledged, raising his hand like he was in court.

"What is it, Charlie?" Hector asked.

"You swear too?" I asked him.

"Sure."

"It's my dad," I said.

Neither of them said anything for a second—they were waiting for me to talk.

"Are you worried about the calculators?" Tommy finally asked. "Is it about that?"

"Worse than that," I said.

"Is it about Career Week?" Hector asked.

I just nodded.

"He's not the president of his company, is he?" Hector asked.

"No," I said.

"I knew that," Tommy said. "But I didn't want to say anything. Why did you tell people he was?"

"I didn't!" I shouted.

"You kind of did," Tommy said.

"I know. But everybody was just bragging so much, and then Robby said numbers were stupid. And then I thought maybe Dad was going to get a promotion."

"So just tell everybody," Tommy said. "It's no big deal."

"Yes it is," I said.

"So what's wrong?" Hector asked.

I took a big breath and let it out. "My dad lost his job on Friday."

"What do you mean?" Tommy asked.

"His stupid boss Mr. Grimaldi told him they didn't need him anymore."

"Is that like getting fired?" Tommy asked.

"I guess so," I said.

Kids were screaming as they went down the slide. A teacher blew a whistle. The soccer game had started without us. I looked out across the

playground and saw a moving van drive down the street. I wondered if we'd have to move away.

"Wow," Tommy said. "That's really bad."

"I know," I said.

It was quiet for a moment. Then Hector said, "My dad lost his job once."

"Really?" I asked.

"When I was five," he said.

"What happened?" I asked.

"He stayed at home for a long time, but finally he found another job. I mostly remember how happy my mom was. After that, we came here."

"My mom lost her job once," Tommy said. "Actually, she quit because she didn't like where she worked."

"But my dad's supposed to come in and talk about his job," I said. "If I'd kept my big mouth shut in the first place, Dad wouldn't have signed up for Career Week. And then I just made it worse when I told everyone how important his job was."

"Yeah," Tommy said. "You really put your foot in your mouth this time."

"What?" Hector asked.

Since Hector's main language was Spanish, sometimes he didn't understand what things meant in English. I guess "putting your foot in your mouth" did sound a little strange to him.

"You know," Tommy said, "putting your foot in your mouth."

"Why would you do that?" Hector asked. "*How* do you do that?"

"No, Hector," I explained. "It means you said something you shouldn't have and now you're in trouble because of it."

"Oh, wait!" Hector said. "I see. It's the same in Spanish, but it's your shoe. *El zapato*. We say '*meter el zapato en la boca*.'" Then he laughed out loud.

"What's so funny?" Tommy asked.

"Because I just remembered one time when I really put my shoe in my mouth."

"What happened?"

"Just listen. I will tell you the whole story."

14

The Wicked Witch of Santiago

"When I was six, we lived in this apartment in Santiago," Hector started. "I walked to school, but in the afternoons school was over before my mother or father got home from work. So I needed a babysitter. They asked this very old woman who lived down the hall if I could stay with her after school. Her name was Señora Velora."

"Señora Velora?" Tommy said. "That sounds like a character in a movie or something."

"She looked like one, too. She had a long, droopy face, and she wore heavy earrings that made her ears hang down and dozens of bracelets on each arm that sounded like chains rattling when she walked. She always carried a cane, but she did not use it very much, except to hit things when she was mad. And she was almost always mad about something. If her mail was late, she swung the stick at the mailman. If the elevator was slow, she smacked her cane against the elevator door."

I was surprised. Hector usually didn't talk very much—this was the most I'd ever heard him say. I looked over at Tommy, and he nodded his head at me. He was surprised, too.

"I had to stay with her every afternoon until my mother got home," Hector went on. "Señora Velora made me sit at the little table in her kitchen and didn't allow me to touch anything. *Nada*. Not one thing. And every day she would give me the same snack. Three crumbly, stale little crackers, always the same kind, and a glass of milk that wasn't even cold. If I didn't drink all the milk, she smacked the leg of the table with her cane."

"Wow!" Tommy said. "That sounds horrible."

"I hated it!" Hector said. "And her apartment smelled really old, too. I was scared of her but I didn't say anything to my parents. And then one day, I saw this show on television about a boy who discovers that the woman next door is a witch. After that, I was sure that Señora Velora was a witch."

"Maybe she was!" Tommy was always ready to believe in witches and ghosts and werewolves.

Hector nodded. "One Saturday morning, my parents had to go to a meeting at the bank and they told me I must stay with Señora Velora. As soon as they opened our door to take me to her apartment, I started to cry. 'I don't want to go!' I said. 'I am afraid of her! She is a witch! *Una bruja!*' My mother told me that she was not a witch, just a nice old lady. 'No!' I screamed. 'She *is* a witch. She feeds me poison crackers and poison milk and she's an evil witch. I don't want to go to her apartment because she will stick me in the oven!'"

Tommy was in hysterics. "Señora Velora—the wicked witch of Santiago!"

"*Exactamente!*" Hector laughed. "My mother told me to stop yelling and be polite, then she grabbed me by the arm and pulled me out the door. And there she was! Señora Velora standing in the hallway with her cane and her drooping ears and her bracelets. She had heard everything."

I gulped.

"Oh, man!" Tommy said. "What happened?

"My mom tried to pretend everything was all right. '*Buenos días,* Señora Velora,' she said. 'I'm just bringing Hector to your apartment.' Well, Señora Velora squinted her eyes, and she raised her cane and pointed at me. I thought she was going to cast a spell on me so I screamed again, even louder. She waved the cane and hissed, '¡*Sinvergüenza¡*'"

"What's that mean?" Tommy asked.

"*Sinvergüenza* means that you're a person with no shame," Hector said. "Like you don't care what you do."

"Seen-ver-gwen-zah!" Tommy shouted.

"What happened?" I asked.

"Señora Velora went back to her apartment and slammed the door. My parents had to take me to their meeting at the bank. I never went back to Señora Velora's apartment again. I was afraid to even look at her. And I felt really bad for calling her a witch. I guess that is really putting your foot in your mouth."

I couldn't believe Hector had done that. I'd never seen him do anything wrong. It was good to know he did dumb things, too.

"That is a disaster," I said.

"A catastrophe," Hector agreed.

"A *dis*astrophe!" Tommy said.

We all agreed. It was definitely a disastrophe.

"I put my foot in my mouth once, too," Tommy said. "In fact, I ate my whole *zapato*."

Hector and I looked at him. "What do you mean?" I asked.

Tommy took in a deep breath and started telling his story.

15

About to Explode

"Remember last summer when my family went on that trip to see the Grand Canyon and everything?" Tommy asked.

"Yeah," I said. "You sent me that postcard of a great big guy riding on a tiny little donkey!"

"Yeah, but I never told you about what happened when we went on this tour out in the desert to see some dinosaur fossils. There were two buses full of people—moms and dads and grandparents and little kids. There was even a bunch of college kids. On the way, the buses stopped at this place where you could buy snacks and souvenirs. The tour guide told us that we had twenty minutes, and he said the most important thing we had to do before we got back on the bus was to go to the bathroom, because it was an hour and a half drive to where the dinosaur fossils were and there was no restroom on the bus. As soon as we got off, my mom told me to go to the bathroom right then before it got too crowded.

"But inside the store I got interested in all these awesome fossils and Native American stuff and about a million other things. Since I only had five dollars, I couldn't afford any of the really cool stuff. I saw a sign that said *Today's Special—Large Soda and Candy Bar Only $3.50,* so that's what I bought. I had just enough money left to buy a piece of fossilized wood, and I got in line to pay for it and drank my soda while I waited. It was a long line and a huge soda. Before I knew it, the guide guy was telling everyone to get back on the bus.

"By the time I finished my soda and paid for my souvenir, everybody else was already on the bus, and my mom came looking for me. She was really mad and yelled at me to hurry up. 'Did you go to the bathroom?' she asked. So I said, 'Yeah' even though I hadn't."

"Uh-oh," I said.

"I know!" Tommy went on. "As soon as the bus started down the road, I had to go. But I thought I could hold it. So I waited, like five minutes, but then *I really had to go!* I kept squirming in my seat, crossing my legs and squeezing them together as tight as I could. I didn't want to tell my mom or dad. Finally my dad asked me what was wrong and I told him 'nothing.'

"'Tell the truth,' my mom said. 'Why can't you sit still?'

"I gave up and shouted that I really had to go to the bathroom. I mean, I was about to explode!"

Hector started to laugh. So did I. I had to go to the bathroom just thinking about it.

"Then what happened?" asked Hector.

"It gets even worse! My dad asks me if I can wait, and I tell him I can't hold out much longer. And Mom's so upset she has steam coming out of her ears. All the people around us are trying not to look at me, because they can see how bad I have to go.

"Just when I think I'm going to die, my dad gets up and walks to the front of the bus and talks to the tour guy and the bus driver. In a minute, our bus pulls over to the side of the road, and the other bus stops right behind us. We're in the middle of the desert. There's no gas stations, no buildings. Not even any trees to hide behind! Dad comes back and says, 'Let's go,' and I moan, 'But everybody's watching. I can't!' and he says, 'Oh, yes you can. This is what you get for saying something that wasn't true.' He leads me down the aisle of the bus. It's really quiet. We get off the bus and there's no place to go, so he takes me a few feet off the highway and I see everybody on both buses looking out the windows at me."

"Oh no!" Hector says.

"Oh yes! Dad turns me around facing away from the buses and says, 'You've got one hundred and twenty people waiting for you, Tommy. Let's get it done.'

"But now I'm so nervous, I *can't* go, even though I really have to!"

"That happens to me, too!" I said.

"Right!" Tommy agreed. "So my dad spreads out his jacket and holds it out to the sides so I'm sort of hidden, but everybody knows what I'm doing. It takes me a while, but finally I finish. When we get back on the bus everybody's smiling at me and an

old guy says, 'It's all right, kid. I know what that feels like.'"

Hector and I were laughing our heads off. The stories were so funny, I'd almost forgotten about the mess I was in.

One of the teachers blew the whistle to tell us to come in. We headed toward the door, still laughing.

I was a bozo, but at least my friends were bozos, too.

◆ ◆ ◆

Sam's dad came in that afternoon. He brought in a bunch of wiring and switches and talked about working in all different kinds of buildings. Dashawn asked if he had ever been electrocuted, and Mrs. Burke said that was an inappropriate question and we should all know better. And then Mr. Marchand gave us all little flashlights with his company's name and phone number on them.

As we were getting in line for the buses, Manny Soares told me he couldn't wait to get a calculator from my dad.

16

Transformation!

Another day went by, and my dad hadn't found a job. One day closer to Friday when everyone would find out I had a really big blabby, fibby mouth. The next day, right before lunchtime, Mrs. Burke said, "Charlie, could you please take to this to the office?"

At least being Master Messenger gave me a chance to think about something else. I took the paper from Mrs. Burke and headed out the door.

I loved being in the hallway, so I thought I'd take the long way around, past the fourth-, fifth-, and third-grade classes. When I passed Mrs. L's class, her door was open.

I stood there, a little to the side where she couldn't see me, and looked for Tommy. He was at his desk working on something. I waved at Colton Burkheiser, who sat next to him, and signaled for him to tell Tommy to look up. When Colton poked him, Tommy glanced over and saw me. He grinned and then started making ridiculous faces. I made faces back. It was hilarious.

"Charlie," a voice said.

"Oh, hi, Mrs. L," I said.

"Are you supposed to be in the hall?"

"I have something to deliver," I said, holding up the paper.

"Well, you'd better do it. I'm sure Mrs. Burke wouldn't be happy to hear you were disrupting my class."

I turned and headed down the hallway.

I was almost to the office when Mr. Turchin came trundling down the hall, pushing a handcart. On top of it was a big plastic and metal thing.

"Hello there, Charlie," he said.

"Hi," I answered, then pointed at his cart. "What's that?"

"A water cooler, you goofball," he said. "What do you think? It's a brand new one and it's going to the teacher's lounge. Hey, do you have time to come along and open the door for me?"

"Sure." I was always happy to help Mr. Turchin. I walked down the hall with him and pushed open the door to the teacher's lounge.

A couple of teachers were sitting at the table. Mr. Romano, my third-grade teacher, was making copies at the copy machine.

"Hi, Mr. Turchin," Mr. Romano said. "Hi, Charlie."

"Hi, Mr. Romano."

Mr. Turchin unloaded the water cooler in the corner and headed out the door. "Be right back with the water jugs."

"What are you doing, Charlie?" Mr. Romano asked. "Practicing to be a custodian?"

"No. Just helping. I'm the Master Messenger in Mrs. Burke's Empire."

"Good for you," he said. "Just like Mercury."

I had learned about Mercury in Mr. Romano's class.

"Yep," I said. "Just like Mercury. Only faster."

Mr. Romano and I talked for a little while, then I told him goodbye and headed toward the office.

I loved being Master Messenger.

"Charlie, where have you been?" Mrs. Finch asked when I got to the office. "Mrs. Burke just called down, wondering where you were."

"I had to help Mr. Turchin," I said.

"Well, you'd better hurry back to class," Mrs. Finch said, taking the paper. "It shouldn't take you ten minutes to make one delivery."

Ten minutes! How does time go by so fast? I nodded and walked out into the hall. Without thinking, I headed back the way I'd come, past the kindergarten, third-, and fifth-grade classes. I didn't run.

Not until I was out of sight of the office.

Transformation!

I was no longer Charlie Bumpers. I was Buck Meson, rocket-powered superhero.

17

King Philip Elementary
Honor Student

At first, I just walked really fast. Then I started to jog. When I reached the end of the kindergarten classrooms, I decided to speed up a little. I looked ahead to make sure no one was coming around the corner. I made the turn.

It was clear.

Time for takeoff! Buck Meson's rockets engaged. I zoomed past the third-grade classes.

I made jet sounds, *"KKKSSSHHHHHHH!"* and switched to my space narrator voice: *Speeding through the sky, delivering messages around the earth in the blink of an eye! No one can believe how fast he goes! How does he do it? No one knows! He—*

Just as I reached the corner to the fourth- and fifth-grade wing, Mr. Turchin came around it, pushing a cart with two big jugs of water stacked on top. I was headed right toward him at full speed!

"Aaah!" I screamed.

"Whoa!" Mr. Turchin yelled. Even though he tried to steer the heavy cart out of the way, it veered right into my path.

I was about to change directions, but the door to a fifth-grade classroom opened up and someone came out.

A fifth-grade teacher. Mrs. Blumgarden.

Oh no!

I barreled into Mr. Turchin's cart and one of the water jugs went flying. It bounced once on the floor and the cap on top popped off. Water shot up in the air.

I slammed into the cart, then went soaring across the hallway, like Buck Meson.

With no brakes.

I flew right into Mrs. Blumgarden, kept going, and hit the wall at full speed. Head first.

KA-BLAM!

The next thing I knew, I was lying on the floor on my back, staring at the ceiling. My head was throbbing. I lifted my head. Mrs. Blumgarden was getting up off the floor. The water jug was lying on its side, making a glugging sound. Water was gushing out onto the hallway floor. My shirt and pants were getting sopped.

Mr. Turchin was scratching his head, trying to figure out what had happened.

"What do you think you were doing?" Mrs. Blumgarden yelled, straightening her blouse.

Trick question! No good answer.

"Flying down the hall like Buck Meson" was definitely not a good answer.

But the truth was, I couldn't answer. My head was all woozy, and when I tried to get up, I felt really wobbly and sat back down. I put my head between my legs and then felt my forehead. Ouch! There was already a huge bump over my right eye.

Meanwhile, water kept glugging out of the jug.

Mrs. Blumgarden and Mr. Turchin were standing over me, looking down.

"Are you all right?" Mrs. Blumgarden asked.

"I think so," I said, trying to act like I was.

But I wasn't.

"Here," Mr. Turchin said, reaching down his hand to help me up. "I think we'd better get you down to the nurse's office."

"I'll take him, Mr. Turchin," she said.

"I'll get the mop," he said, turning the water jug right side up.

"What's your name?" she asked me.

"Charlie. Charlie Bumpers."

"Bumpers. Are you Matt's brother?"

"Uh-huh." I was still feeling pretty woozy.

"This is what happens when you run in the hall," she said in the way grown-ups talk when they want to teach you a lesson.

I had never heard of anyone else knocking themselves out running into a water jug, but I guess she was right.

Mrs. Blumgarden walked with me down the hallway, her fingers wrapped tightly around my arm. It might have been to make sure I didn't fall. It might have been to make sure I couldn't escape.

By the time she got me to the nurse's office, I was feeling a little better. She left me there with Mrs. Veazie, the school nurse, who sat me in a chair and put an ice pack on my head.

"It looks like you've got an egg growing out of your forehead," she said. "That's quite a bump. And your clothes are all wet. What happened?"

"I'm not sure," I said.

"Really?" she asked, sounding concerned. "You don't remember?"

"I think I ran into a wall," I said. "And also a teacher."

"Okay, that's good," she said and smiled.

I didn't know what she meant by "good." I guess

she thought it was good I remembered what had happened.

My disaster.

My catastrophe.

I was sitting there on the edge of the cot when the door opened and someone walked in.

Mrs. Burke.

Complete disastrophe.

I waited for her to yell, but she didn't.

"What happened?" she asked.

"He got a bump on his head," said Mrs. Veazie. Which was almost a perfect answer, since it didn't say what really happened.

"It sounds like more than that," Mrs. Burke said, giving me a meaningful look. "Are you going to be all right?"

"I think so," I said.

"Okay then," she said, "I'm sure Mrs. Veazie will take good care of you." Then she left. It felt like there was a lot more to say. And a lot of it I didn't want to say or hear.

Mrs. Veazie did a bunch of tests. She shone a light in my eyes and asked me to follow her finger as she moved it back and forth in front of my face. Then she asked me what my name was and a few other things about where I lived. After I'd answered all her questions, she said, "Well, I think you're fine. Except for that bump on the noggin. You'll probably have a headache. You'll need to stay here until I can call your parents."

"I'm really okay," I said. I didn't want to have to explain to Mom and Dad what had happened.

"We always notify the parents in cases like this. And just to be safe, we will have to keep an eye on you for a while."

She found a T-shirt and a pair of pants and some underwear for me to wear. I guess she kept extra clothes in case someone threw up all over themselves.

Or maybe in case someone knocked over a water jug and a teacher and hit a wall with his head.

The T-shirt she gave me said "King Philip Elementary Honor Student" on the front.

I don't think I deserved that.

Mrs. Finch stayed with me while Mrs. Veazie made the call.

When she came back, Mrs. Veazie said she'd talked to my mom.

"Is she mad?' I asked.

"Worried," she answered.

I sat in the nurse's office for an hour, wondering what my parents were going to say.

Mr. Turchin came by to see if I was alive.

"You made a heck of a mess, Charlie," he said.

"I'm sorry," I said.

"There's no use crying over spilt water," he said,

chuckling to himself. I was glad he wasn't mad. I knew Mrs. Blumgarden was.

I wished I could go back to class. I didn't want to miss lunch and recess.

Just when I thought I couldn't stand it anymore, Dad walked in.

"Hey," he said. "Are you okay?"

How come *he* was here instead of Mom? Did they let him out of work to come get me?

Then I remembered. Dad didn't have a job anymore. But right then, I didn't care. I was just glad to see him. I could almost feel myself wanting to cry, but I held it in.

"You must be Mr. Bumpers," said Mrs. Veazie. "I'm Vicky Veazie, the school nurse."

"Yes, nice to meet you. I think I'll take Charlie home for the rest of the day, if it's all right."

"I'm sorry you had to leave work," Mrs. Veazie said.

"No problem," my dad answered.

"Just sign him out at the office," she said. "Keep an eye on him, and don't let him take a nap until bedtime. If you notice any problems, you should call your doctor."

I stayed in the nurse's office while my dad went down to the classroom and got my backpack and homework assignments from Mrs. Burke. We said goodbye to Mrs. Finch and Mrs. Rotelli, and Dad put his arm around me and led me out the door to our car.

I was going to miss Ellen's mom talking about web pages, but I was kind of relieved we were going home. That way I wouldn't have kids asking me again about my dad being president of the company and how many calculators they were going to get.

That afternoon I was glad that my dad wasn't the president of anything. For a little while, he could just be my dad.

18

The Kid Who Knocked Over Mrs. Blumgarden

When Tommy got on the bus the next morning, a smile spread across his face. He plopped down on the seat next to me.

"How are you?" he asked.

I pulled my hair back and showed him the bump on my head. It was red and swollen and the skin above my eye was turning purple.

"Gross," he said. "But awesome. Everybody's talking about it!"

"Talking about the bump on my head?"

"No. About how you knocked over Mrs. Blumgarden and Mr. Turchin's cart and spilled a hundred gallons of water in the hallway. All the kids in her class saw it!"

"I don't think it was a hundred gallons," I said.

"Whatever." Tommy shrugged. "You're famous! The kid who knocked over Mrs. Blumgarden. You'll go down in school history!"

I put my head in my hands. This was turning into the worst week of my life. Every teacher in school was going to hate me.

"You'd better hope that you don't get Mrs. Blumgarden next year. This is worse than hitting somebody in the head with a sneaker."

"Thanks for reminding me." I had hit Mrs. Burke in the head with a sneaker in third grade. Totally by accident. And this *was* worse.

At school, the kids in the hallway all stared at me.

When I got to my classroom, it was quiet, and kids were doing their morning work. Mrs. Burke, the Ruler of the Empire, was at her desk.

"Are you all right, Charlie?" Hector whispered as I sat down.

"Yeah." I showed him the bump on my forehead.

"It's what you get for running in the hall," said Samantha Grunsky, the most annoying human ever.

"How do *you* know I was running?" I asked, even though I knew she always knew everything.

"Because you knocked over Mrs. Blumgarden."

Just then Mrs. Burke called out, "Mr. Bumpers, come up here, will you?"

Uh-oh.

I walked up to her desk. She put her pen down and looked at me. "How's your head?" she asked.

"Okay," I said. "It's still sore."

"Mrs. Blumgarden told me about your little accident," she said.

"Uh-huh," I said.

I figured Mrs. Burke had a lot more to say, but she wasn't saying it. She seemed to be waiting for me to speak up.

"I was late getting back from the office," I said. "I was kind of running."

"I thought so."

"I'm sorry," I mumbled.

"I don't think I'm the one you should be apologizing to. Why don't you go down the hall and talk to Mrs. Blumgarden?"

I really didn't want to, but Mrs. Burke just sat there looking at me with those teacher eyes you cannot escape.

"Go right now before classes start," she said. "And do not run."

I walked down the hall to Mrs. Blumgarden's room. The door was open, so I went in. All the fifth graders looked up and saw me. Mrs. Blumgarden was writing an assignment on the board.

"Um, excuse me…" I wasn't sure what to say next.

She led me out the door into the hallway. At least I didn't have to apologize in front of her whole class. That would be almost as bad as going to the bathroom in the desert in front of two busloads of people.

"How is your head?" she asked me.

"Not too bad," I said. "It still kind of hurts, though."

"I'm sure it does," she said. "You hit the wall pretty hard."

"I'm really sorry I knocked you over, Mrs. Blumgarden," I said. "I shouldn't have been running. I was hurrying to get back to class."

"I accept your apology," she said. "Let's not let it happen again, all right?"

"Okay," I said. "Are you all right?"

"I was just very surprised," she said. "It was like a rocket hit me."

I nodded. It *was* a rocket. But I didn't say that.

When I got back to class, Mrs. Burke called me to her desk again.

"One more thing, Charlie," she said. "Because of what happened, I'm afraid you're going to lose your job as Messenger. We'll have to let someone

135

else do it for the rest of the week."

"But, Mrs. Burke—"

"No buts, Charlie."

"Yes, ma'am."

My dad and I had both been fired!

I headed back to my seat, trying not to look at the big smile on Samantha's face.

◆ ◆ ◆

That afternoon Mrs. Burke asked Dashawn to take over as Master Messenger. Then she sent him to the office to bring Tricia's dad back to our classroom.

Everybody saw I wasn't the Messenger anymore. I felt sick inside.

"I knew this would happen," said Samantha.

"It's okay, Charlie," Hector whispered.

Tricia's dad came in carrying a big box. We all knew he worked for a company that made sports equipment, so we were eager to find out what was in it.

Mr. Davidoff told us that his job was to convince stores and websites to sell the things his company made. He set up a slide show and showed pictures of him shaking hands with all these different sports stars—football, basketball, baseball, hockey, tennis—everything. There was even a picture of Tricia standing next to a soccer player who had played on the Olympic team. The kids were so excited they couldn't stay in their seats.

Until Mrs. Burke snapped her fingers. *POW!*

As Mr. Davidoff's presentation went on and on, I felt sicker and sicker. My dad hadn't met any sports stars. He'd never introduced me to anyone famous. And all the time, everybody kept asking what was in the box, and Mr. Davidoff kept saying to wait.

Finally, when it was almost time for the last bell, he opened the box.

"Now, I've got a little something I asked my company to make for you." He reached into a big plastic bag and pulled out a cloth stretchy thing.

It was a bright blue headband.

"Awesome!" Alex yelled. He was the first kid to get one. "Look what it says!"

Embroidered across the front of the band were the words, ***Mrs. Burke's Empire.***

Everybody put one on. Even Mrs. Burke, which looked pretty funny.

"What do we say to Mr. Davidoff?" Mrs. Burke asked as Tricia's dad headed out the door.

"Thank you!" everyone yelled.

"Wait until tomorrow," Alex said. "Charlie's dad will be here with his calculators!"

"I never said that!" I shouted. But no one heard me. They were all cheering. Hector looked at me. I just shook my head.

Maybe I could find a way to stay home sick tomorrow. I sure felt sick right then.

19

An Ignoramus the Size of Mount Everest

When the Squid and I got home from school, I walked Ginger and then went up to my room. Mom had to work late and wouldn't be home in time for supper.

I must have been in really bad shape because I did my homework right away.

I hardly ever do that.

Then I lay on my bed and tried to read a book. I couldn't pay attention to what I was reading, so I just stared at the ceiling.

Finally, Dad called us down for dinner. He had made grilled cheese sandwiches. We all sat down at the kitchen table and started eating.

I love grilled cheese, but I didn't even taste it.

I had other things on my mind. Had Dad found a job? Had he found any extra calculators? What was he going to say when people asked him about his work?

But most of all, I wondered what I was going to say when everyone found out that I hadn't been telling the whole truth. I hadn't exactly lied. I just hadn't said what was really happening. And by the time I'd tried to say it, nobody was listening.

Finally, I couldn't hold it in any longer.

"Dad?"

"Mm-hmm?" he mumbled. He was looking at his phone, which he never does at dinner.

"Did you talk to anybody about a job today?"

As Dad looked up from his phone, Matt excused himself and walked out of the kitchen.

"Yes, Charlie," Dad said. "I made a few phone calls."

"Did someone say they would hire you?"

"Not yet," he said.

"I'd hire you, Daddy," the Squid said.

"You can't hire anyone," I told her.

"Yes, I can," she said. "I'm hiring Daddy as my daddy. I'm going to pay him a million dollars."

Dad smiled and let out a long sigh. "Thanks, Squirt."

Then I heard Matt's voice calling from upstairs. "Charlie, come here a minute!"

That was weird. My brother never called me. "I'll be right back." I hurried out, leaving Dad and the Squid sitting at the table. Matt was waiting for me at the top of the stairs. When I got there, he turned and headed toward his room. He stopped at his door and motioned for me to go in. I walked past him.

"Sit on the bed," he said, closing the door.

"Why?" I asked.

"Just sit there for a minute, will you?"

I could see that Matt was really mad. What was wrong? I didn't think my brother would ever actually beat me up, although sometimes he would get me down on the floor and pin my arms down and beat on my chest with his fingers like a drum. But that was just to make me mad. This was different.

I sat on the bed. He stood in front of me.

"You've got to stop it," he said.

"What?"

"Stop bothering Dad about his job. You're being a complete jerk."

"But I just want to know what's going to happen. I—"

"Charlie, shut up for a second!"

"You're not supposed to tell me to shut up!"

"And you're not supposed to be a moron. How do you think Dad feels?"

"What do you mean?"

"How do you think he feels about losing his job? Do you think he's happy?"

"No."

"Do you think he likes not working?"

"No. But—"

"Do you know what it feels like to lose a job?"

Actually, I did. I'd lost my dream job just that afternoon. I wasn't the Master Messenger anymore and it felt horrible.

"I only—"

"Stop it!" he said. "Dad feels worse than we do! He's the dad! He's supposed to know everything, and he doesn't right now. Your dumb questions are making him feel worse."

I opened my mouth to say something, but no words came out. I didn't know what to say—everything was confused and confusing. Dad was always Dad—he was always all right. Sometimes he got mad or upset, and I remembered how sad he was when Grandpa Al died. But Dad was always the one who tried to make things okay.

"I didn't mean to make Dad feel bad," I said in a shaky voice. "I just don't know what to do."

"About what?"

"About him coming into my class tomorrow."

"Big deal! Maybe he doesn't come in. So what?"

"But he said he would. And I told Mrs. Burke—"

"Charlie, you're an ignoramus the size of Mount Everest! Dad speaking to your class is just one dumb little thing. If he wants to come in, okay, but don't bug him about it anymore. He's got other things to think about."

"It's just…"

"What? What's so important?"

I blew air out of my mouth. I could feel tears in

my eyes, and I REALLY didn't want to cry. "It's just...well, some of the kids think he's, like, the president of his company and—"

"What? Why do they think that?"

"And everyone thinks he's going to bring in a calculator for each kid in the class."

"Did you tell them that?"

"No!" I moaned. "They just decided that. And I couldn't say it wasn't true until it was too late. And then I was hoping maybe Dad would get to be a vice president or—"

"SERIOUSLY?" Matt was towering over me. I tensed up, ready for him to pin me on my back and drum on my chest with his fingers.

"Or something like that," I went on. "I figured a vice president would have a lot of calculators. And now Dad doesn't even have a job. What's he going to do? What if we don't have enough money? Will we have to move? And the kids are all going to know, and they'll think I was bragging about something that wasn't even true."

I wiped my eyes before tears came out.

Matt sat on the bed next to me.

"You," he said slowly, "are an enormous bozo."

"I know," I blubbered.

Then we sat there for a while. I wiped some snot off my nose.

"Don't rub that on my bed," Matt warned.

I rubbed it on my pants. "I didn't mean to make Dad feel bad," I said.

"But you did," Matt said.

That made me feel worse.

"It's all right, Charlie," Matt said, putting his hand on my shoulder. "You're just a dumb fourth grader."

I slid off Matt's bed without saying anything and went into my room and closed my door. I curled up on my bed and put my pillow over my head.

I lay there like that for a long time. I kind of wanted to see Dad, but I didn't know what to say to him. Or how to say it.

I must have fallen asleep, because I woke up to the sound of my door opening. I kept the pillow on my head—it seemed safer that way. Someone sat on my bed. I could tell it was Dad. He didn't say anything. So I just stayed where I was with the pillow on my head. I wondered if I could just keep a pillow on my head for the next two or three days. If they made me go to school, I could just tape a pillow to my head so I couldn't see anyone or hear anyone. That way if people were looking at me or talking about me I wouldn't even notice. I would just be Charlie Bumpers, the Boy with the Pillow Head.

"Can you breathe?" my dad asked.

"Sort of," I muttered.

He tugged on the pillow, and I let go so he could pull it away.

"Do you want to tell me what you're doing?" he asked.

"Nothing," I said. Which was true.

We sat there for a little while. It was getting kind of boring, but I was still trying to think about what to say. Finally, I couldn't take it any longer. "I didn't mean to make you feel bad," I said.

"I know," Dad said.

"I just want to know what's going to happen."

"So do I," he said.

Aren't dads *supposed* to know what's going to happen? Isn't that their job? What happens when dads don't know?

"What will you do in my class tomorrow?" I was kind of hoping that we could both call in sick.

"Oh, I've got some ideas," he said.

"What?"

"It's a surprise. Just because I don't have a job doesn't mean I've forgotten how to add and subtract."

That was true.

"Dad," I blurted out. "Some kids think you're a millionaire and the president of the company and are going to give everyone a calculator."

He sat there for another minute not saying anything, then he leaned over and gave my hand a squeeze. "It'll be all right," he said, standing up. "Put your pajamas on and get under the covers. See you in the morning."

So I did. When I got in bed, I put the pillow back over my head. Just in case.

A couple of minutes later, I heard the door open. I peeked and saw Mom come in. I think she was checking on me. But I didn't move and pretended to be asleep. She leaned over and kissed me on my shoulder. "Good night, Charlie," she whispered.

I still didn't move.

Then she left.

20

Waiting for the Helicopter

Tommy sat down beside me the next morning on the bus.

"Did your dad find a job?" he asked.

"Nope," I said.

"Is he still coming to talk to your class?"

"I guess."

"What's he going to talk about?" Tommy asked.

"I don't know," I said. "He told me not to worry."

"Is he going to hand out calculators?"

"Nope," I said again.

"Your dad's funny," he said. "Maybe he'll just crack jokes. Maybe he'll get a job as a comedian."

"Ha ha ha," I said.

◆ ◆ ◆

Kids kept coming up to me in class to ask me questions like "Hey, Charlie, is your dad coming to school in a limousine?"

When Robbie asked me if my dad was bringing in computers for everyone, Samantha Grunsky said, "Charlie's dad isn't rich. He's not giving out computers."

I kind of wish my dad *would* give out computers, just to bug Samantha. Her mom and dad were both lawyers—they would probably hand out laws for us to follow.

At lunch, Tommy and Hector and I sat at a table in the far corner of the lunchroom, but other kids still found me. First, Alex and Trevor came over and started asking what kind of calculators my dad was bringing. Then Kyle and Darren showed up with big smiles on their faces. "Hey, Charlie," said Darren. "When's your dad taking you on vacation in his private jet?"

"We don't have a private jet," I said. "I've never even been on an airplane!"

All of a sudden, Tommy stood up.

"STOP IT EVERYBODY!" he shouted.

Everyone at our table quit talking and looked at him.

"Listen, you guys!" he said, loud enough for the whole cafeteria to hear. "Charlie's dad is not a millionaire. He's just a thousandaire."

Everyone stared at him like he was out of his mind. I'd never heard of a thousandaire before—I figured he just made that word up.

"What's a thousandaire?" Darren asked.

"Someone who has a thousand dollars, you dummy," Tommy explained. "Duh!'

It was quiet for a minute, then Alex started giggling. Trevor joined in, and pretty soon they were all laughing. I didn't feel like laughing myself, but I was glad when Kyle and Darren gave up and went back to their table.

◆ ◆ ◆

At recess, I decided to shoot baskets by myself, hoping no one would find me. But as I was dribbling the ball over to the basket, Tracy Hazlett ran up to me.

"Hi, Charlie," she said.

"Uh…hi," I stammered. My hair tingled and my ears felt all hot and sweaty.

"Your dad's coming in today, right?"

"Uh-huh," I said.

"Okay. Don't forget what you said about saving a calculator for me."

"Um, okay. It's just—"

Before I could say anything else, she turned and ran back across the playground.

With everyone reminding me, I thought, *how can I ever forget?* I shot at the basket and didn't even hit the rim. The ball hit the backboard and bounced off to the right. I chased down the ball and dribbled it back to take another shot.

Mrs. Burke was standing right where I'd started shooting. Where did she come from?

"How come you're not playing soccer?" she asked.

"I didn't feel like it," I said.

"Are you excited about your dad coming this afternoon?"

"I guess." I dribbled a couple of times, then shot the ball, and it bounced off the rim right to where Mrs. Burke was standing. She caught it but didn't pass it back. She just held the ball.

"Do you want to tell me anything?" she asked.

"Not really," I said, hoping she would just give me the ball back. I wished people would stop talking to me all the time.

"Are you sure?" she asked. She dribbled the ball once.

"It's just—"

"Just what?"

Boogers. I had to tell her.

"Me and my big blabby mouth."

"What did your big blabby mouth do?" she asked.

"I sort of let everyone think that my dad was a big shot in his company...and...and now my dad doesn't even have a job."

She frowned. "Really?"

"Yeah. He lost his job last week, but he said he'd still come in. And because of my big mouth everybody thinks he's, like, the president of the company and he's going to bring in free calculators."

Mrs. Burke bounced the ball again. Then she passed it to me. I caught it. She held out her hands like she wanted it back, so I bounced it back to her. Then she took a shot at the basket.

It went right through the hoop, hit the ground, and spun back to her. "Your turn," she said, passing it to me.

We took turns shooting the ball without talking.

After a while, she looked at her watch. "Time to go in," she said. She blew her whistle and we both started walking back toward the school door.

"Hang in there, Charlie," she said. "Things have a way of working out."

◆ ◆ ◆

After recess, our class was fidgety and much noisier than usual. I thought Mrs. Burke might say

157

something to calm the kids down, but she didn't. She didn't even snap her fingers when Sam got up to look out the window. He told her he was waiting for the helicopter that was bringing my dad.

Now it was 1:45 and we were doing silent reading, waiting for my dad to show up. The phone on the wall by Mrs. Burke's desk buzzed. She picked it up and turned her back to us so we couldn't hear what she was saying. Then she hung up. "Citizens," she said. "I have some bad news for you."

All the kids were already quiet, but we got even quieter.

"I just got a call from Charlie's father..." She paused.

So it *was* about my dad! What had happened? Now I was really worried.

"He just called to tell me that something has come up and he can't make it today."

"Oh, no!" Alex wailed. "No calculators!"

POW! Mrs. Burke snapped her fingers.

"But," she said, "he knows you were looking forward to his visit and so he's asked a friend to come instead."

A friend? Who was my dad sending in his place?

Just then there was a knock on the classroom door.

Mrs. Burke went to the door and opened it.

A weird-looking man walked in.

21

"Noombers Are Bee-yoo-ti-ful Things"

The man was wearing a white lab coat. The chest pocket was stuffed with pencils. He was wearing a wig with crazy white hair that stuck out in every direction. And black-rimmed eyeglasses with a big nose attached.

"Hel-looo, most excellent peoples!" the man said in a very strange accent. An accent I'd heard before.

Then I realized who it was.

My dad.

A couple of kids laughed.

"I oonderstand thees ees Meez Burke's Empire, and you are learning about different jobs. My dear friend Meester Boompers ees away, on other planet, and so I am happy to talk about the work of noombers. My name ees Professor Zed."

"Where's Charlie's dad?" Joey Alvarez called out.

POW! Mrs. Burke snapped her fingers again.

Dad grabbed his chest like he'd been shot. "Ow!" He looked down, checking for a wound. "Oh, good, I am not eenjured. But please to raise hands, so no one ees harmed. And as for your question, Meester Boompers ees fine, just fine, thank you. He sends his regards."

A bunch of hands shot up in the air.

"No questions, please!" my dad said. "Hands down, hands down. So math genius can theenk."

But Alex still had his hand up, waving it around.

"What?" my dad asked, looking at him.

"Did you bring in calculators for us?"

"Calculators! You want calculators? We don't need no steenking calculators. Already I have one!" He put his fingers on the sides of his forehead and closed his eyes. "My brain ees beeg calculator. I show you."

He whipped a marker out of his pocket. "Five noombers in the hundreds, please, from 100 to 999. Queekly!"

He called on five kids.

"Four hundred thirty-seven," Candy said.

"Two hundred ninety-three!" Manny called out.

"Seven hundred and ninety-nine!" Dashawn yelled.

"Three hundred thirty-three," Lydia said.

"Nine hundred sixty-four," Cory said.

Professor Zed wrote each number up on the board, one under the other. Then he drew a line at the bottom and added a plus sign. I knew what was going to happen. I'd seen my dad do this before.

"Someone watch the clock and say go!" He pointed to Alex. "You, boy who wants calculator. Tell me when to go."

Alex jumped out of his seat, he was so excited. "Ready, set, go!"

My dad looked at the numbers for about three seconds. Then he wrote 2818 on the board in big numbers.

"How do you know?" asked Alex.

"Because of my brain calculator. Meez Burke, please check total."

Mrs. Burke got out her calculator and punched in the numbers. "You're right!" she said, holding it up so the class could see.

"That was lucky!" Sam said.

"Luck! Noombers not about luck! Noombers are bee-yoo-ti-ful things, like flowers in spring. Try again."

The kids gave him more numbers. Dad did the trick twice more, and he seemed to get faster each time.

By now the kids had forgotten about my dad. As far as they were concerned, this was Professor Zed speaking.

"You're just doing a trick," Trevor said.

Dad turned toward him. "A treeck? You want a treeck? I show you treeck. Treeck anyone can do. We will mooltiply any noomber by nine. What is nine times forty-three?

No one answered.

The professor placed his fingers on his head and closed his eyes. "Three hoondred and eighty-seven."

"Right," said Mrs. Burke, looking up from her calculator.

"Another noomber?" Dad looked over at Mrs. Burke. "Ees okay to not raise hand?"

She nodded.

"Nine times sixty-four!" someone yelled.

"Five seventy-six," Dad said without hesitating.

"Right!" Mrs. Burke said, a big smile on her face.

Kids kept calling out numbers and Dad kept multiplying by nine, and no matter how big the number, he kept getting the answer right away. Then he showed us how he did it.

"First mooltiply noomber by ten, which ees just adding a zero. For example, ten times sixty-four ees six hoondred and forty. Then you subtract the original noomber—six hoondred forty minus sixty-four ees five seventy-six."

Dad spent the next ten minutes doing one kind of trick after another. Everyone knew he was my dad, but they kept calling him "Professor Zed" like he was a real person.

"Now, any questions?" he asked.

Trevor asked him how he knew all the things he'd showed them.

Before Dad answered, he took off the wig and

the fake glasses and the lab coat.

Now it was just my dad.

"I knew all along it was Charlie's dad," Samantha announced.

"Duh," Robby said, "everyone knew it was Charlie's dad."

"Hey, Mr. Bumpers? How'd you get so smart?" Taleeah Dawson asked.

"I love numbers," Dad said in his normal voice, "and the ways they make sense. I've always loved working with them."

"No wonder you're president of your company with all the things you can do," Trevor said.

"I heard you had a plane!" Sam crowed.

Uh-oh.

Mrs. Burke stood up, ready to take charge. But my dad looked over at her and held his hand up, as if to say it was okay. Mrs. Burke nodded, then went to the back of the class and sat at an empty desk. Dad turned to face everyone.

I held my breath, afraid of what he might say.

"Well," he said, "I heard some of you thought I might be the president of a company and fly all around the world on my private jet."

A couple of kids nodded.

"And hand out calculators to everyone," Alex said, still hoping it was true.

"Well," Dad said, "the truth is, right now I don't have a job."

Everybody fell quiet. Half the class turned to look at me, and I looked down at my desk.

"Why not?" Manny asked.

I gulped.

"Because," Dad said, "the company I worked for made some changes and let some people go. I was one of them. Sometimes things like that happen."

"But Charlie said you were president," Sam said.

Now everyone was staring at me. I had never really said that, but I still was really embarrassed.

Then Hector spoke up. "No, he didn't," he said. "Everybody else said that, but not Charlie. Nobody listened to him when he tried to explain."

Then everyone started talking all at once.

"Hold it, hold it," my dad said, raising his hand. He sounded just like he did when Matt and I started arguing at the kitchen table. Everybody settled down and looked at my dad. With Mrs. Burke sitting at a desk in the back, it was like Dad was teaching the class.

"Everybody exaggerates, and sometimes we go a little overboard. I'm not the president. I don't have a jet. Right now, I don't have a job. But I'm still Charlie's dad. And I still love numbers."

Carmen Torres held up her hand. My dad nodded at her. "Yes. Do you have a question?"

"I have a connection, Mr. Bumpers."

"Okay, go ahead," Dad said.

"My dad didn't have a job when I was in second grade," she said.

"My mom had to leave her job last year," Sarah Ornett volunteered. "When my grandma got sick, my mom stayed home to take care of her."

Dad called on three or four other kids, and each one had a story about someone in their family or neighborhood who had lost their job.

We all blinked in surprise when Mrs. Burke raised her hand. In her own Empire!

"Yes, Mrs. Burke?" Dad asked, like he had conquered the world and was the new Emperor.

"The truth is," Mrs. Burke said, "my husband lost his job a few years ago, and it took him a long time to find a new one. But now, he's very happy with his new career."

Wow. This was unbelievable. Even Mrs. Burke's husband!

"Mr. Bumpers," Alex said, "I think you should be president of a company. You're really smart."

My dad broke into a huge smile. "Thank you, Alex. Before I go, Professor Zed has one more thing to show you." Everybody leaned forward, waiting to hear what he had to say. He put the wig back on, along with the glasses and the big nose, then turned to Mrs. Burke. "Meez Burke," he said in his funny accent, "you have very smart class. I know they want calculators."

A few kids started applauding.

Had my dad actually found some to give out?

"But after I show you theese leetle treecks, you know the best calculator ees brain. So I have calculators to make brains grow beeger."

What was he talking about?

Dad walked to the door, stepped out into the hallway, and pushed a handcart into our room. On the top shelf was a box that looked a lot like the one Maria's mom had brought in from her bakery. He wheeled the cart to the front of the class.

"So," Professor Zed went on, "I brought in calculators. But! They are not calculators to put noombers in, since already noombers are in your head. I ordered calculators from bakery. They are calculators to eat and feed the beeg calculator brain you already have."

He reached in the box and pulled out a rectangular object about the size of a cell phone. When he held it up, you could see it was a cookie. But the icing on it made it look just like a calculator.

"Calculator cookies!" he said. He took a big bite. His eyes grew wide. "Already I am smarter!"

Everybody cheered and clapped. Dad pushed the cart up and down the aisles, handing a cookie to each kid. And one to Mrs. Burke.

"Charlie!" Alex crowed. "Your dad's a genius."

Kids lined up to give me high fives.

Even Samantha Grunsky!

"I like your dad," she said. "No wonder you're not horrible at math. He probably checks your homework."

I didn't say anything. He did check my homework.

I was lucky he did, and I knew it.

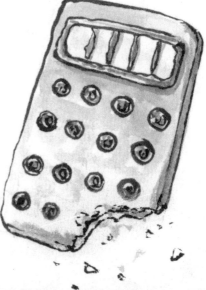

◆ ◆ ◆

There was only half an hour left before school was over, but Dad said he needed to go. Everybody thanked him and I followed him out into the hallway.

He smiled at me. He was holding the wig and glasses and lab coat in his arms.

"How'd we do?" he asked.

"Great, Dad," I said. "Thanks."

"Are we okay?"

I nodded. "Can I go home with you now?"

He shook his head. "No, you go home on the bus. I've got some errands to run."

Then he grabbed me and lifted me up in a giant bear hug.

"Ah! My guts!" I said.

He put me down again. "See you at home later, Charlie."

"Bye, Dad," I went back inside the classroom, where kids were still eating cookies and talking about Professor Zed.

22

A Little Happy Dance

When the Squid and I walked in, Matt was already home, sitting at the kitchen table reading Komodo Man, a comic book about a guy who can turn into a giant killer lizard. Ginger barked and jumped up on me, which she is not supposed to do. She was dying to go for a walk.

"Where's Dad?" I asked.

"Dunno," Matt said, not looking up from the comic book. "You're supposed to walk Ginger."

"I know."

Matt looked up. "How was Dad?" he asked.

"Dad didn't come," I said.

"What? I thought he was—"

"Professor Zed showed up instead."

"Who's that?" asked the Squid.

"Some friend of his."

"I didn't know Dad had a friend named that," the Squid said.

"Neither did I."

I thought I'd keep it a secret between Dad and me. Before they could ask me any more questions, I put Ginger on the leash and took her outside to walk around the block. I ran most of the way, hoping that Dad would be back by the time I got home.

He wasn't. But Mom was in the driveway, getting out of the car.

She handed me a bag of groceries to carry. "Where's your father?" she asked as we went into the kitchen.

"We don't know," the Squid said. "Charlie told us he didn't even come to talk to Charlie's class. He's disappeared."

"Dad didn't come?" Mom said with a concerned look on her face.

"No," I said. "Someone else came in his place."

"Who was it?" the Squid asked. "Mom, make Charlie tell us."

Just then the back door opened. Dad came in with his Professor Zed costume under his arm and a big envelope in one of his hands.

"Daddy!" she squealed, wrapping her arms around his waist. "Where were you?"

"Oh, just checking up on something." He had a smile on his face, like he was keeping a secret. Maybe a bigger secret than Professor Zed.

"Who came to Charlie's class?" Matt asked. Now even he was interested.

"Old friend of mine," Dad said, putting on the nose and glasses. "A professor I know."

The Squid shrieked with laughter. "Did you wear that?" she asked.

"Yep," Dad said. "And this," he added, putting

on the wig. The Squid laughed even more.

"I'm just glad you didn't come to *my* class wearing that," Matt said.

"Funny you should say that." Dad paused, grinning at Matt.

"I don't like the sound of this," Matt said. "I don't need you to visit any of my classes."

"After I left Charlie's class," Dad said, "I got to thinking about how much I loved math, and how much I enjoyed talking with kids."

"Everyone really liked you," I said. "Even Mrs. Burke."

"So," Dad continued, "I went down to the school office and talked to Mrs. Rotelli. I told her I thought I might be interested in teaching."

"Teaching? Where?" The Squid got up from the table and started doing a little happy dance around the kitchen.

"I don't know yet," Dad said. "There's a bunch of things to take care of. I drove over to the school offices and talked to people there. I'd have to take some classes and get a teaching certificate. It will take a while. But it looks as if I would probably qualify to be a substitute teacher for the rest of the school year."

"You could substitute if Mrs. Diaz was sick!" the Squid shrieked. "Sometimes Mrs. Diaz gets sick! Once she told us she even threw up! And you could be my teacher!"

"Or Mrs. Burke!" I said. The kids would love having Professor Zed come in again.

"Well, I actually talked to them about teaching middle school math," Dad said, turning to smile at Matt.

"What?" Matt squeaked.

"You wouldn't mind, would you?" Dad asked.

Now Mom was smiling. "Perfect!" she said.

Matt's eyes opened wide. "My father teaching at my middle school?" he whispered. "This is a nightmare!"

Mom and Dad started laughing, and so did I. The Squid was still skipping around doing her happy dance and Ginger was barking like she thought it was funny, too.

Matt was shaking his head, but I could tell he was trying not to smile.

"I'm going to tell everybody," the Squid said.

"I'm not telling anybody," I said. "Not yet."

Who knows what might happen when you open your big, blabby mouth?

BILL HARLEY is the author of the award-winning middle reader novels *The Amazing Flight of Darius Frobisher* and *Night of the Spadefoot Toads*. He is also a storyteller, musician, and writer who has been writing and performing for kids and families for more than twenty years. Harley is the recipient of Parents' Choice and ALA awards, as well as two Grammy Awards. He lives in Massachusetts.

www.billharley.com

ADAM GUSTAVSON has illustrated many books for children, including *Lost and Found*; *The Blue House Dog*; *Mind Your Manners, Alice Roosevelt!*; and *Snow Day!* He lives in New Jersey.

www.adamgustavson.com

Don't miss the other books
in the Charlie Bumpers series—
Charlie Bumpers vs. the Teacher of the Year,
Charlie Bumpers vs. the Really Nice Gnome,
Charlie Bumpers vs. the Squeaking Skull,
Charlie Bumpers vs. the Perfect Little Turkey, and
Charlie Bumpers vs. the Puny Pirates

Also available as audio books.

: 978-1-56145-732-8
978-1-56145-824-0
: 978-1-56145-770-0

HC: 978-1-56145-740-3
PB: 978-1-56145-831-8
CD: 978-1-56145-788-5

HC: 978-1-56145-808-0
PB: 978-1-56145-888-2
CD: 978-1-56145-809-7

HC: 978-1-56145-835-6
PB: 978-1-56145-963-6
CD: 978-1-56145-893-6

HC: 978-1-56145-939-1
PB: 978-1-68263-001-3
CD: 978-1-56145-941-4

And watch for the seventh book
in the series, coming up soon!